Close Encounters
of the Snarkian Kind

Close Encounters of the Snarkian Kind

A Portmanteau inspired by Lewis Carroll's
The Hunting of the Snark

by Byron W. Sewell

ILLUSTRATED BY
THE AUTHOR

evertype
2016

Published by Evertype, 73 Woodgrove, Portlaoise, R32 ENP6, Ireland. *www.evertype.com*.

A catalogue record for this book is available from the British Library.

ISBN-10 1-78201-134-X
ISBN-13 978-1-78201-134-7

Typeset in De Vinne Text, Mona Lisa, ENGRAVERS' ROMAN, *Liberty*, Warnock Pro Light, *Commercial Script*, and Didot by Michael Everson.

Illustrations: Byron W. Sewell.

Cover: Michael Everson, based on a design by Alan Tannenbaum and Byron W. Sewell, after the 1977 poster for Steven Spielberg's film.

Printed by LightningSource.

For my lovely and talented wife,

Victoria

Foreword

"Close Encounters of the Snarkian Kind" was originally written and privately posted by Byron W. Sewell to a few of his Carrollian friends for their entertainment, in the Victorian manner of issuing a story one chapter at a time. The initial "part" eventually became Chapter I of the story published here. The next week Chapter II appeared, continuing the story. That was well received and this continued until there were eventually a total of four chapters and Byron thought that he was finished with the story. However, Alison Tannenbaum wrote Byron, requesting another chapter or two. In response, Byron wrote a fifth chapter, entitled "A Posy for Alison", and the story was finally concluded with Chapter VI. There was no original plot, list of characters, etc. Each chapter simply fed off of what had occurred in the previous chapters. Byron claims that he was surprised as anyone about the ending. That is not the way most people are taught to write a story. It's just how his mind works. The main character in this science-fiction tale is the psychopathic murderess, Dayna Keiner. She is named after a well-known Canadian Carrollian, not because she is also a psychopath, but rather out of simple friendship and fun, and because at one time her name was Dayna Nuhn, and Byron took her surname as a pun on the German word "keiner", meaning "none".

The title of Chapter I, "Subtle Azzigoom", is a quotation from Lewis Carroll's novel, *Sylvie and Bruno*, which reads:

"How blest would be
A life so free—
Ipwergis-Pudding to consume,
And drink the subtle Azzigoom!"

No one knows exactly what Azzigoom is.

That's the sort of silliness that pervades some of these stories. The reader will find numerous allusions to other famous modern-day Carrollians in many of his stories. See how many you can identify!

"Polka Dot Snark" was inspired by the name of a high school in the West Virginia town of Poca, located in Putnam County, the same county in which the Sewells live. Poca High School is locally famous for their mascot, the "Dot". According to Wikipedia, this was a reference made in 1928 during a football came, when a reporter exclaimed, "they look like a bunch of red polka dots running around the field!"

That's almost as funny as the true West Virginia town name of Big Bottom, briefly mentioned in "The West Virginia Snark Hunting Society". Byron says that he first became aware of the name when he saw a poster in a storefront window that said: "REVIVAL! Big Bottom Baptist Church". ("Bottom" here refers to a river bottom, not a congregation of Baptists with prominent posteriors.) The reader will often find West Virginia locations in Byron's stories, some of which Evertype has already published, including *The Carrollian Tales of Inspector Spectre*.

Michael Everson
January 2016

Contents

Feeding the Boojum

Feeding the Boojum

I

Stevenson and his Samoan guide, Tofilau, a very pleasant and soft-spoken young man in his mid-twenties, left the little port of Olosega on Olosega Island late in the morning, heading north along the old coastal road to Sili, with Tofilau holding the reins of a small packhorse with their necessary supplies. It was a typically beautiful day in the Manu'a Islands, part of the island chain in the Western Pacific known collectively as the Navigators' Islands. The temperature was perfect, the azure sky was filled with fair-weather clouds, there was a steady, balmy breeze, and the Pacific was resplendent in myriad shades of blue.

Looking west across the narrow Asaga Straight that separates the little islands of Ofu and Olosega, Stevenson drank in the tropical beauty of Ofu and its twin volcanic peaks, their steep sides covered in lush jungle all the way down to white sandy beaches.

Stevenson had hired Tofilau in Olosega the evening before, having arrived from Upolu aboard the private yacht *Gabeln und Hoffnung*. Tofilau was native to Ta'u, the largest of the three Manu'a Islands. He spoke an adequate version of broken English and was, of course, fluent in the dialect of Samoan spoken by the islands' ordinary inhabitants. Stevenson felt confident that he was in good hands.

After a few hours of casual walking they reached the outskirts of what had once been the willage of Sili, without having encountered a single soul on the road that was now largely overgrown from disuse. The survivors of a major typhoon that had roared through the islands a few years earlier had abandoned the village, most relocating to Olosega or Ta'u. Sili, situated on the northern side of the island, had been very exposed and vulnerable to the high winds and torrential rains.

Stevenson knew that Sili had been hard hit by the typhoon, but he had nonetheless expected to find a few people still living there, and was surprised to find that, apparently, the only person left was the old man they could see burning something on an ancient stone altar platform. He seemed oblivious to the bluish-white smoke swirling around him, stirred helter-skelter by the breeze.

"Is he a priest?" Stevenson asked Tofilau, nodding in the direction of the old man.

"He *ali'i*. Maybe he priest; I no sure. One time he high chief in Sili. No more people live here now. Typhoon kill many, many. House gone. Shrine blow away. Some people live, go Olosega. Some go Ta'u. He live here alone now. Make sacrifice."

"Is he sacrificing to Tagaloa-Lagi, the Great God?"
"Yes."
"What might he be sacrificing?"
"Maybe he burn chicken. Maybe breadfruit or coconut. Me think he pray to *moa*, too."

Stevenson misunderstood him. "To Moses? Is he also a Christian?"

Tofilau laughed softly. "Not *Moses*; *Moas*. *Ali'i*, he not Christian! *Moa* is ghost. Many people die in typhoon. Many people long time die in volcano. So, many *moa* stay here. Sili now bad-bad place. Full of ghost. No one want live here no more. Afraid.".

"When did the volcano erupt?"

Tofilau thought for a moment, struggling to remember a date he had once been told. "Grandfather tell me something. I think maybe 1860. Something like that. Volcano blow away this side of Ofu and Olosega." He pointed towards the steep cliffs in the sides of the mountains on Ofu that formed the sides of a caldera, whose bottom would be somewhere out in the Pacific stretching to the north.

"Yes, I see," Stevenson said. "Do you really believe in *moas*, Tofilau?"

"Of course! *Moa* real. Very dangerous. Eat you."

Stevenson had to suppress a laugh; Tofilau seemed so serious. "Do you know of anyone who was ever eaten by a *moa*?"

Tofilau thought about this then admitted that, "No, but me sure *moa* eat peoples."

"How do you know?"

"Everybody know. Little children know. My parents tell me. Parents no lie. They say *moa* real. They all time hungry. Eat people. Eat children if they go outside alone at night."

Stevenson decided to let it drop. "Come, let's go over and talk to the *ali'i*," Stevenson said as he started to go in that direction.

Tofilau grabbed his arm and firmly restrained him. "No go! Him dangerous. Strong. Everything here *tapu*—taboo! Sacrifice *tapu*. Altar *tapu*. Smoke, too, *tapu*."

"Why is the smoke taboo?"

"Smoke carry prayer to Heaven. Smoke sacred."

He had no sooner said this than the wind suddenly shifted, blowing sacred smoke in their direction. Tofilau bolted, but the smoke overtook him. Stevenson, whose tubercular lungs were extremely delicate, was also engulfed and he immediately started coughing violently.

The startled chief, who had apparently been in a trance while he prayed, whirled around at the sound of Stevenson's loud coughing. "*Asu sa!*" he screamed. "*Sa! Tapu! Tapu!*" Gesturing wildly with his hands, he screamed, "*Alu! Alu!*"

Tofilau ran back and grabbed Stevenson by the arm, forcibly dragging him back down the road, trying to put some distance between them and the irate, hysterical *ali'i*. "Hurry! We go now. Danger! He say smoke sacred. *Tapu.* Hurry! We run! Run fast."

Stevenson could do nothing except cough, his lungs screaming in agony. He began to cough up specks of bright-red blood.

The chief quit shouting at them and began chanting. Between coughs Stevenson managed to ask Tofilau, "What is—the *ali'i*—saying?"

"He sing curse." Tofilau looked absolutely panicked. "Now we die."

"Nonsense!" Stevenson said. "That's just superstition. Come on—let's leave as fast as we can. I'll try to hurry, but my lungs are on fire. Exactly what is he saying?"

"I no know. Him chant in *tatala lele*. Me not chief man. Me no understand most *tatala lele* words. Me speak *tatala leaga*. But I tink he sing curse. Bad curse." Then he repeated, "We die." Tofilau suddenly dropped to his knees, as if surrendering to whatever his fate would be; as if it was sealed and there was absolutely no escape; no point in even trying.

Stevenson ran about twenty yards back down the road, this time trying to lead the way himself. "Come on! Come on!" he yelled back to Tofilau, but Tofilau didn't move, oblivious to Stevenson's pleading.

Then Tofilau suddenly screamed, *"Moa!"*

To Stevenson's utter amazement he saw that a pillar of swirling black smoke had collected a few feet above the platform, towering eight or nine feet into the air. As he watched, it formed itself into a monstrous, animal-shaped thing, and then, a few moments later, it flew with astonishing speed, engulfing the still-kneeling Tofilau, who screamed in excruciating agony and then collapsed. To Stevenson's horror the blackness then began to move in his direction and he distinctly saw what appeared to be large red eyes, glowing from within the smoke near the top, where a head might be imagined. Stevenson turned and ran for his life, glad that at least the road was downhill. A hundred yards further on he heard the packhorse scream pathetically and then abruptly go silent, and instinctively he knew that the hapless animal was now also dead.

Stevenson ran, coughing terribly as he fought for breath, blood dribbling down his chin from a haemorrhaging lobe. It occurred to him that he might well die, drowning in his own blood as it filled his lungs. But the threat of the *moa* seemed much worse, so he ran; better to drown than to be consumed by whatever was chasing him.

An hour later, completely exhausted, he stumbled into Olosega and made his way down to the waterfront to see if, by the slimmest of chances, the *Gabeln und Hoffnung* might still be in port. To his immeasurable relief it was, and he got as far as the dock before collapsing. The captain saw him fall and calling his small crew to help, they collected Stevenson's limp body and got him back aboard ship and into a berth.

A few minutes later Stevenson had recovered enough to talk briefly with the Captain in between fits of bloody coughing.

"What happened?" the Captain asked.

"My guide, Tofilau, and I accidentally stumbled into a taboo area in the remains of Sili. An old headman was there making a sacrifice and when we accidentally got into the smoke from the sacrifice he cast a curse over us. Some sort of demonic spirit materialized in the smoke over the altar and killed Tofilau, as well as our packhorse. I ran for my life. I believe that it is still hunting for me and that I am in grave danger!"

"A demonic spirit?" the Captain asked, thinking that Stevenson must be hallucinating, perhaps from a fever.

"Tofilau called it a *moa*."

The Captain laughed. "A *moa* is a ghost, man! Are you saying you saw a ghost? *Moas* are just superstitions; they aren't real. It's like the Bogeyman. Parents tell their children about *moas* so they will behave."

"Well, if not a ghost, then perhaps it was a Boojum."

"A Boojum?"

"A kind of snark."

"A kind of what?"

Stevenson didn't try to explain. "Look, I will pay you fifty pounds to set sail immediately for Upolu. I need to see a doctor. My lungs are haemorrhaging. I may not live long without attention."

The Captain nodded. "Done," he said. "You just rest. Don't move any more. Try to let your lungs heal enough to quit bleeding. We'll get you to Upolu in record time."

I I

A full moon had risen several hours earlier, its bright, pearly light in the nearly cloudless sky transforming the dark waters of the Pacific into what appeared to be an ocean of quicksilver and bathing Upolu in a kind of luminous twilight.

Exhausted from the mental strain of dictating another installment of *Weir of Hermiston* to his wife, Fanny, Stevenson had gone out to sit on one of the high-backed rattan chairs strewn up and down the second-floor veranda that ran along the entire front of Vailima, his palatial home on the hillside high above the small harbor of Apia, some four kilometres distant. He loved the view and relished the humid air in the breeze that came up the hillside from the sea, gently stirring the dense forest that surrounded their house into a soft, leafy whirr, and comforting his delicate, inflamed lungs. The moonlight was so bright that it was quite possible to read the headlines on the German newspaper on the small end table beside his chair, though the eye-strain was hardly worth reading weeks-old news. It had been a happy, productive day, and, in spite of the tiredness that had finally overwhelmed him, he was contented.

Fanny emerged through the bedroom door in a swirl of long skirts with two brandies and sat down in the matching chair beside him. "Here you are, my dear," she said softly, handing him a snifter. He smiled and then placing his nose inside the glass breathed in the heavy bouquet before taking a sip.

"Perhaps we will only need another six installments and then *Hermiston* will be finished," he remarked. Glancing up, he was startled to see what looked like a dark shadow materializing at the northern end of the veranda; an oddly-shaped, hulking blackness that swirled slowly, as if composed of smoke. Strangely, it absorbed every silvery ray of moonlight that struck it. At first he thought he might be experiencing a migraine. He took off his glasses and wiped them carefully with the handkerchief he kept in his pocket. Quickly replacing them, he stared across Fanny's left shoulder at the sinister form now moving slowly towards them. A moment later he saw two large eyes, the size and shape of papayas, near the top of the apparition, deep red and glowing through the blackness.

Fanny noticed his wide-eyed stare and the frightened look that had come across his thin face. "What is it, dear?" she asked, turning in her chair to see if she could see whatever it was that he was looking at. She saw nothing except the normal furniture on the veranda. She turned back to her husband and asked again, "What is it, Robby? What do you see?"

"It's the *moa*—the Boojum!" he whispered, his voice barely audible.

"What did you say, dear? The 'Boojum'?" She turned back to look again, but saw nothing.

"From Sili—on Olosega," he continued in a hushed voice. "Oh, my God! What is it doing here? It's not supposed to be on Upolu! How did it find me?"

As it came closer he jumped to his feet, holding his right arm stiffly outstretched, as if to hold it at bay, but it was a futile gesture. The blackness engulfed him. He screamed in excruciating pain, pressing his palms against his temples, then abruptly collapsed, knocking over the small table. The snifter shattered.

Fanny screamed and dropped to his side. When it was obvious that he was unconscious she got back to her feet and rushed over to the banister. "Malavai!" she screamed. "Tagiilima! Come quickly up to the veranda! Come quickly! Tusitala is ill!" She returned to his slumped body, dropping to her knees again and then gently lifted his head onto her lap, tears streaming down her cheeks. She gently pushed his dark, shoulder-length hair back from his face

A few minutes later the two servant women rushed through the bedroom door. "Malavai," Fanny instructed, "quick, saddle the horse and ride as fast as you can down to Apia and fetch Dr Artz. Tell him Robert has had an attack and is gravely ill. Ask him to please hurry! Ride as fast as you can!" she repeated. Malavai turned and rushed from the room.

Fanny turned to the other woman. "Tagiilima, help me get him into bed."

Even though Robert was rail-thin, it was all they could do to drag him into the bedroom and lift him up onto the high four-poster bed.

Stevenson lived several more hours, but never regained consciousness.

Dr Dietrich Artz arrived thirty minutes later, and confirmed that Stevenson had died. He listened as Fanny briefly described what had happened, and then told her, "I feel certain that he suffered a massive stroke; a cerebral haemorrhage. There was nothing that any of us could have done for him. I'm very sorry."

Several days later they buried him on the hillside behind Vailima, the gravesite having a spectacular view of the ocean and the little harbour of Apia.

After the simple graveside service Fanny sought out Dr Artz and asked him to accompany her into the library. "I have something that I believe Robert would have liked you to have."

"Of course," he said and they walked silently back to Vailima and into the library.

Fanny picked up a thin volume from the desk and handed it to him. "This was one of Robert's favourite books," she said. "It's a nonsense poem by the English author Lewis Carroll. Have you heard of him?"

"But of course; the author of *Alice's Abenteuer im Wunderland*. It was one of my daughter's favourite stories when she was young. I read it to her many times and know it well."

"This one is entitled *The Hunting of the Snark*, written years after the *Alice* books. Have you ever read it?"

"No, I am afraid that I have not heard of this one."

"Robby had it rebound in a design of his own making." She handed it to him.

He looked at the spine. "But this has the title *Feeding the Boojum*. I thought you said *The Hunting the Snark*."

"I'll try to explain. The poem is about an improbable quest for imaginary creatures called 'snarks', of which one particularly unsavory type is known as a 'boojum'. On one page, that Carroll intended to be a completely blank map, Robby drew the outlines of two of the Manu'a Islands. Here, let me show you." He handed her the book and she opened it to that page, and then returned it to him. "Robby believed that those picturesque islands were just the place to find a snark, and he even went so far as to travel there on his own childish quest for the mythical creatures. He had such a wonderful, child-like imagination.

"However, something terrible happened during his exploration of the islands and he returned very distressed and very ill. He almost died from his lungs haemorrhaging. He would never tell me exactly what happened. A few months later he had the book rebound as you see it, with the revised title on the spine."

"Yes, these are unmistakably two of the Manu'a Islands: Ofu and Olosega. They have very distinctive shapes. I have also been there, though I must admit that I did not hear any talk about snarks or boojums. I see that he has written the word '*Boojum*' next to the abandoned village of Sili."

She nodded. "I haven't told anyone else exactly what happened the night Robby died, but I think you should know. Can you keep what I am about to tell you in strictest confidence?"

"Of course."

"That night he saw something terrifying on the veranda where we were sitting. I heard him say in a whispered, frightened voice that it was 'the Boojum'. He was obviously very

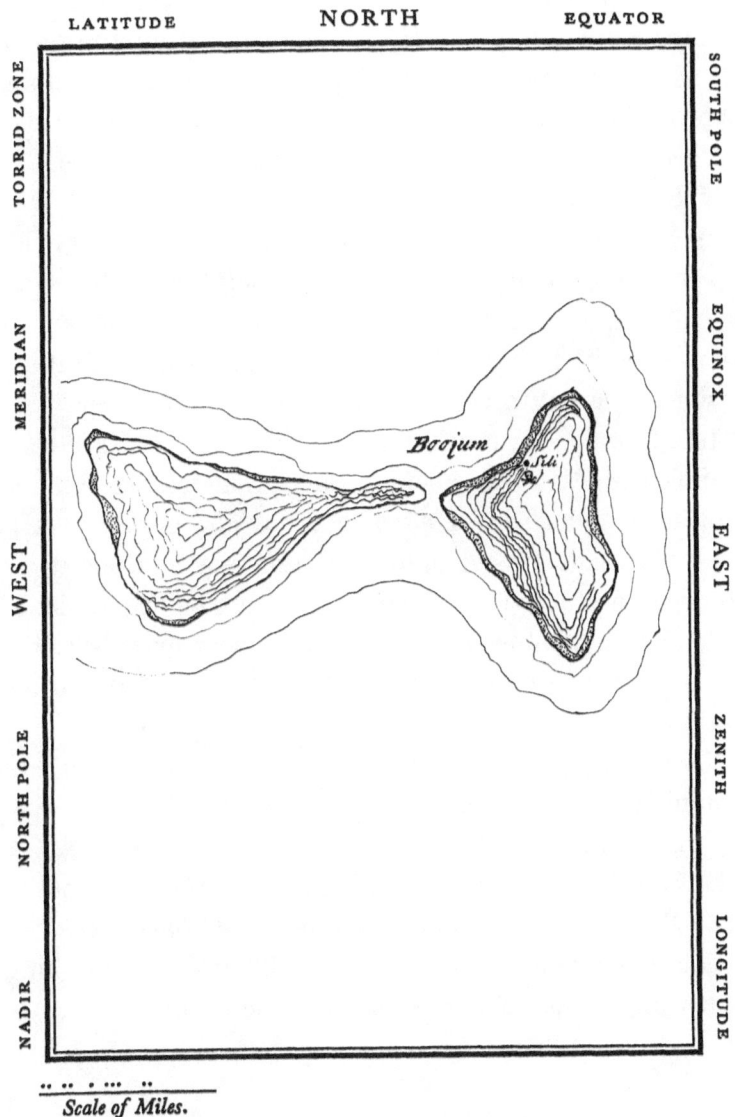

frightened by whatever he saw. I looked at where he was staring, but I could see nothing unusual. I'm not at all sure if it was just in his mind or if he was actually seeing a ghost; or perhaps his death angel. He suddenly stood up and put his arm out, as if to protect himself, and then screamed, grabbing his head, in terrible pain. Then he collapsed."

"This is very strange," Dr Artz remarked. "Perhaps it was a vivid delusion triggered by the stroke."

"Perhaps; I don't know. It obviously seemed very real to him. Anyway, because of the association, I don't want the book in the house; it would always remind me of his death. Would you like to have it? I hate to throw it away or burn it and it's too personal to simply give away to a servant or stranger."

"Yes, I would very much like to have it." He closed the book. "Thank you, Mrs Stevenson. It is a great treasure, which I shall always cherish." He reached out and gently took her hand, which he kissed lightly. "I am very sad about your terrible loss. Forty-four is much too young an age to die. The world has been immensely blessed by your husband's writings and is greatly impoverished by his sudden and untimely passing. "

"Thank you, Doctor. I know that you did all you could humanly do to arrive in time to help Robert. I will always be very grateful to you."

"But I was too late. I did nothing. In fact, there was nothing that I—or anyone else on the island—could have done."

"You came when I called for you. That was something I greatly appreciate. You have been a true friend."

I I I

*I*n 1914, when war broke out, Germany abandoned her colony of Western Samoa, and its colonists, including Dr Artz, departed on the first available boats leaving Upolu for Europe. Eight weeks later he finally arrived at his family home in Vienna, having made his way tortuously through Turkey and Bulgaria. Another two months later found him in an army field hospital on the Western front, where he miraculously survived the entire war. Tragically, in 1918 he contracted influenza and died a week later. His personal effects, including *Feeding the Boojum*, which he had left in Vienna inside a vault, were inherited by his sole-surviving relative, Hans Belmann.

Six months after the signing of the Armistice, Belmann traded *Feeding the Boojum* to Akiva Kupner, an antiquarian book dealer, for half a loaf of bread, in a dire attempt to fend off imminent starvation. It kept him alive for an additional week. He died standing in a long soup-line.

Many years later, *Feeding the Boojum* was purchased for 40 francs from the Kupner estate by François Boucher, a French book dealer who was in Vienna on holiday. Boucher returned to his home outside Paris, where the book remained until 1946 when he sold it to Private Jon Hood, an American soldier stationed in Paris.

Two days later, while walking along the embankment of the Seine opposite the Notre-Dame, Boucher drowned when he dived off of the bridge into the river under very suspicious circumstances. One witness related to the police that he heard Boucher scream and, turning to see what was happening, watched in horror as Boucher backed up, as if fighting off some invisible attacker, and then jumped over the balustrade.

What seemed peculiar to the police was that Boucher was reputedly an excellent swimmer.

Six months later, Private Hoode returned to his hometown of Selma, Alabama after his discharge from the Army with *Feeding the Boojum* tucked into his single piece of luggage.

I V

*T*homas Baker answered the phone. "Mr Baker?" The voice was unfamiliar, with a pronounced German accent.

"Speaking."

"Ah, Mr Baker! Excuse me for interrupting you. We have never before met. My name is Hutmacher; Helmut Hutmacher. I am calling from New York City. I believe that I might have a book of interest to you."

"What's the name of your bookstore?"

"Hutmacher Rare Books. I deal in only extreme rarities. By appointment only. From my home."

"How did you get my unlisted phone number?"

"From Edward Gross, who is an antiquarian book dealer in Zürich and from whom you have purchased certain Dodgson rarities in the past. Yes?"

"Yes, I know him. Why would he give you my confidential number?"

"I asked him for it. I heard that you are a prominent collector of Lewis Carroll with a special interest in *The Hunting of the Snark,* and as I did not have your number to contact you, I called my colleague, Herr Gross. We sometimes refer clients to each the other. It is not every collector who can afford this book."

"So, are you offering me a *Snark*?"

"Yes. A quite remarkable copy of the first edition."

Baker seriously doubted that he would be interested, since he already owned five different varieties of the first edition, including two inscribed by Dodgson to child-friends, one bound in red and the other in green. "What's so special about this one?"

"For one thing, it has been unusually rebound and—"

Baker cut him off. "I'm not interested. As a general rule I don't buy rebound books. Thanks for calling, though."

"But wait! I have not described it completely yet. Please, allow me a few of your minutes. I think that you may change your mind."

Baker hesitated and then relented. After all, one never knew when something good might fall right into your lap. "All right. Two minutes. I'm busy."

"Yes. I'm sorry for disturbing you. Please forgive me. The book, it is rebound in black morocco, stamped in platinum with the Jolly Roger. It is very rare to use such a valuable metal in binding a book."

"A skull and crossbones?"

"Yes."

"You aren't going to tell me that it was once owned by a pirate are you?"

"No, no. Of course not! Though you are close, perhaps. It was at one time the property of Robert Louis Stevenson. You have heard of this Scottish author?"

"Of course! The author of *Treasure Island*."

"Yes. He is widely collected. Like Carroll. Signed copies of books from his personal library demand very high prices. In this copy his signature is inscribed in full on the front free endpaper; not just the more common 'R.L.S.'. It has been authenticated by Sotheby's. I can provide documents for your verification."

Baker's interest perked up a bit. "When was it rebound?"

"This is not exactly certain, but I am confident that it is late Victorian—definitely not modern."

"What condition is it in?"

"Unfortunately, only 'minus-good'. The covers are somewhat worn and scratched. There is some foxing of the endpapers and edges. Corners bumped. There is a little damp-staining on a few pages. But the binding is solid. The hinges are not separating."

"How much do you want for it?"

"Twenty thousand."

"Dollars?"

"Yes, of course. U.S. dollars; not Canadian."

"If I can verify what you have said I might be willing to pay you *two*."

"The price is firm. I think you would change your mind if you were to see it."

"I seriously doubt it. Thank you for calling, Mr Hutmacher."

"Wait! I have not told you the most interesting part. You might find it worth my asking price."

"I can't imagine."

"You know the famous blank map, no doubt?"

"Of course."

"This one isn't the blank. It has two islands drawn on it, by Stevenson himself. I have had this handwriting authenticated as well."

"Which islands?"

"Two of the Manu'a Islands, in what is now known as American Samoa: Ofu and Olosega. In Stevenson's time they were part of what was known as the Navigators' Islands."

"Why would he do that?"

"There is no way to know, of course, but I must conclude that they had some great significance to him. There are a few very interesting annotations, and I wonder if perhaps it mightn't be a real treasure map."

"As in *Treasure Island?*"

"Exactly."

"You have a very vivid imagination, Mr Hutmacher."

"Perhaps. But what if I am right? But I am not making this claim. I don't know. It is just a possibility. There have always been rumours of a trove of rare black pearls buried somewhere on Olosega. Perhaps this map reveals their location."

"Seems unlikely. Didn't Stevenson die in Samoa?"

"Yes, in 1894, from a stroke. He is buried on Upolu. Do you wish to buy the book?"

"I doubt it, but send me a scan of the cover and the map and I'll think about it?"

"I will send you a scan of the cover, yes, but not the map."

"Why?"

"If you want the map you must buy the book. You may visit me in New York and see the map, but I will not make you photocopies or scans. No."

"Why not?"

"In case the map is the key to a hidden treasure of black pearls."

Baker laughed. "You're serious, aren't you?"

"Quite. If I were not so old I would travel there and see for myself what might be found."

"Exactly how old are you, if you don't mind my asking?"

"I don't mind. This year I am eighty-three."

"You're right. You're too old to go adventuring. Look, I'll be in the City on business in three weeks, on the Monday. I can drop by and take a look at it. Would that be convenient?"

"All right. But you might be too late."

"Why?"

"At my age I could die in the next few minutes. Three weeks is a long way off when you are gasping for the next breath—maybe too long. Who could know?"

"Try to hold out for a few weeks. What's your address?"

"512 East 86th Street."

Baker thought for a moment. "That address sounds familiar. Do you happen to know a Mrs Jurist?"

"Yes. Janet is my neighbour. A gracious and attractive woman. Do you know her?"

"We've met a few times at LCSNA events. I visited her apartment once when the Society met in New York."

"Really? I didn't know this. Perhaps if you do not desire the *Snark* then she may be the interested. Does she also collect Lewis Carroll?"

"I think at one time she had a small collection of rare curiosities, like some early Chicken Little Press editions. That sort of thing. But I don't think that she's what you would consider a serious collector."

"So maybe twenty thousand might be more than she would be willing to pay for a *Snark*?"

"I have no idea. You'll have to ask her."

"I will do this the next time she brings me soup for lunch."

"She brings you soup for lunch?"

"Sometimes, when it is very cold outside. She thinks maybe I don't take very good care of myself and don't eat so good. She is an excellent cook. Mr Jurist was a lucky man."

"I've never had the pleasure of experiencing her cooking. All right, I'll see you in three weeks, then."

"*Nach Gottes Willen.*"

V

Three weeks later, Baker made his way up 86th Street to Hutmacher's apartment building. He rang the intercom and waited for five minutes. He noticed that there was a small sign on the glass in gold letters for Hutmacher Rare

Books. Just as he was about to give up and leave, the intercom squawked at him. "Who is it?"

"Thomas Baker. We have an appointment at ten."

"A moment, please."

A loud buzzer sounded. Baker pushed open the front door and stepped into a small entryway. He looked at the directory and found Hutmacher's apartment number and went up. He knocked on the door and listened as no fewer than six deadbolts were slowly retracted and the door finally swung open. "Come in, Mr Baker, please," said an ancient-looking man. Hutmacher wore thick glasses and had almost no hair; just a few wispy strands over his ears. He wore a crumpled blue suit and an ancient silk tie patterned with tree frogs and soup stains. "Sorry to take so long. I do not move so fast these days." They shook hands. Baker went inside and Hutmacher closed the door, then bolted three of the locks.

"You must have a serious burglar problem," Baker observed.

"Yes. Because of drugs. No one is safe nowadays. They will kill you for a lousy cigarette!" Hutmacher led the way down a hallway and then turned into a cluttered office with low shelves along three of the walls, most half-filled with old books, many in elegant bindings. Framed maps and some Edward Lear parrot prints covered the walls above the cases. Hutmacher gestured towards a Chesterfield in front of his large desk. "Please—sit," he said as he made his way around the desk and then, completely out of breath, collapsed into a large banker's swivel chair. Baker sat down in the uncomfortable old chair. "Please—give me a minute," Hutmacher said. "My lungs are not so *gut* any longer."

"Take your time, Mr Hutmacher. I'm in no hurry."

"*Danke*," Hutmacher said as he reached under the desk and came up with an oxygen mask connected to a bottle under the desk. He breathed hungrily for a few minutes. "Emphysema," he said when he had finally gotten his breath back. "It is a terrible way to die. A slow death."

"Were you a smoker?"

"No, I am not an idiot who wants cancer. I was once a printer. The solvents did this to me. I quit and became a bookseller twenty years ago, but the damage was already done to my lungs." He opened a desk drawer and took out a pair of white cotton gloves, which he tossed at Baker. "Please put these on if you want to handle the book."

While Baker slipped them on Hutmacher produced a Solander case, from which he removed a thin black volume and handed towards Baker. "I must warn you that this book is cursed. At least three previous owners have died violent deaths. Merely touching it might bring you harm. Do you still want to touch it? I can't be responsible if something happens."

"I don't believe in curses," Baker said as he took the book casually. He examined the striking binding and immediately noticed the title on the spine. "But this doesn't say *The Hunting of the Snark*," he remarked, pointing at the spine and holding it up for Hutmacher to see.

"I know. It is one of its many mysteries. Perhaps Stevenson had it bound like that as a joke. Who can know? The title is rather ominous, I think. *Feeding the Boojum*. But, as you can easily see, the text block is the normal one for *The Hunting of the Snark*. The original blue-green covers are bound in at the back."

Baker flipped to the back to see the covers. "I've never seen this particular colour. I've heard of it, of course, but the blue and green bindings are scarce."

"It may have been a trial binding. I prefer it to the drab brown that Dodgson selected. Perhaps the brown was cheaper. To me the blues and greens are better. They look like the ocean."

Baker opened it to the front and examined Stevenson's signature. Before coming to New York, he had gone on the Internet and studied several examples of Stevenson's signature, and this one appeared to be genuine. It would take an expert to tell for sure. He flipped to the title page and confirmed that it was a true first edition.

"Please, now look at the map," Hutmacher urged.

Baker flipped over to it and found that it was just as Hutmacher had described it to him. He had also taken time to look at a map of American Samoa before coming to New York and saw immediately that these were obviously the two islands Hutmacher had said they were. Curiously, Stevenson had written the word *"Boojum"* next to Sili. "Lots of people with dirty little hands have handled this book," Baker observed. "Perhaps Stevenson's children?"

"No, it could not have been his children. He didn't have any. The fingerprints might be unfortunate for the book collector, but for me it is part of the book's charm. One wonders whose prints they might be. They could be professionally cleaned, of course, but it would be shame to remove Stevenson's prints."

Baker flipped through the book. There were numerous marginal scribbles: strange names and symbols. The rear free endpaper was covered in small almost illegible writing that would take time to decipher. He couldn't recognize the languages, and even one of the alphabets—which he assumed was probably Samoan—he had never seen. "Do you know Samoan?" he asked.

"Only a few words."

"How about this one? *Taumualua*. It's written above the line that says: *'The bowsprit got mixed with the rudder sometimes.'* Any idea about that one?"

"Yes, that one I happen to know."

Baker waited for a moment, expecting him to tell him. He finally asked, "Well, what does it mean?"

"Oh. You wish to know? I didn't understand. *Taumualua* means 'two bows'. It is the name of a kind of ancient boat that they made. It looks something like a modern whale boat and is also propelled by oars. Either end can be the bow. It can be steered in either direction."

"Are you serious?"

"Quite serious."

"That's very interesting! I wonder if Dodgson had that in mind when he wrote this famous line?"

"Who can know such things? But Stevenson obviously thought so. I suppose it is possible. The libraries in Oxford hold many strange things. I would not be surprised to learn that they had an early Samoan-English dictionary or two."

"But Holiday didn't illustrate the boat like that. His boat looks more like a tall ship; perhaps a schooner."

"Maybe Dodgson just gave him a free hand."

"Do you know the meanings of any of the other words in the annotations?"

"I just sell the books. I do not research obscure articles for the Lewis Carroll Society's journals. I am not a librarian or a graduate student. You can find Samoan dictionaries for sale on the Internet and look them up for yourself."

"All right. Don't get upset. I was just asking." Baker dropped the subject and examined the binding a bit closer and saw that it had been expertly done; worthy of a future Sangorski or Sutcliffe. The small, rather shallow ruby set in a silver mount in the skull's right eye socket caught the light and sparkled, giving one the impression that there was something alive inside the book—looking out at the viewer. Sadly, the setting in the left eye socket had been smashed.

"So, Mr Baker—are you interested in buying the book?" Hutmacher asked.

"I'm trying to decide if I would prefer to own your *Snark* or a new car."

"If you are a serious collector then you will prefer the book. Cars you can get anywhere. This book you can get only here. It is unique. A once-in-the-lifetime opportunity. If you must struggle with such trivial financial decisions as the asking price, then you may be out of your league, and should stick to collecting ordinary editions that can be obtained for a mere few thousand dollars."

"Look, I once paid $60,000 cash for an 1865 *Alice*. You needn't worry about my finances. The question is whether your *Snark* is worth what you're asking for it. At the moment I doubt it. Your pitch that it might contain a treasure map is silly, at best. My guess is that if there ever had been a treasure of black pearls then someone has already found it, and some wealthy matron has them on a string in her jewellery box or wall safe."

"Of course there is no guarantee of treasure. I am a bookseller; not an adventurer."

"A book this expensive demands provenance. I've never read or heard anything about a copy bound like this. I'm confident that it has never been sold at auction. There would be records of that and I would have found them. How do I know it isn't a forgery or fake?"

Hutmacher opened a file folder and produced a letter on Sotheby's letterhead. "This authenticates that the Stevenson signature and that a number of other writings in the book are genuine in Stevenson's hand. They agree that this copy has never appeared in the major auctions." He then handed Baker another letter. "This is from Mr Edward Wakeling, editor of Dodgson's diaries. You know him, I suppose?"

"Yes, of course. Anyone who seriously collects Carroll knows who he is. I've corresponded with him a number of times."

"Then you will no doubt recognize his signature?"

Baker nodded as he took the letter. "Yes, this is his handwriting. It's quite distinctive and always written in violet ink."

"Violent ink?"

"Not 'violent'; violet! It's a shade of purple! Like the small flower by the same name."

Hutmacher laughed so hard that he had to put his oxygen mask back on for a minute before he could continue. "Oh! I see! Yes, that is quite a difference!" He laughed again. "Such ink would give the whole new meaning to the words 'letter bomb'!" He burst out laughing again, and needed more oxygen before continuing. "Here you can read that I sent Wakeling a scan of the binding. He confirms that a copy of the *Snark* bound in this manner is unknown to him. That covers the U.K. If it had ever been in England he would know about it. He knows everybody who can spell the name 'Dodgson' on that famous island and has examined every one of their collections; even the Queen's, no doubt."

"Does the Queen collect Carroll?"

"How should I know? But if she does, Wakeling will know about it!"

He then produced a number of other letters from the folder, which he handed to Baker, one at a time. "This one is from Alise Wagner. As you no doubt know, she and her friend Udo Pasterny, the famous German chef, wrote the German *Alice* bibliography. I understand that he keeps his vast collection in his kitchen where it is always close to hand. Neither of them knows anything of it either. That covers the rest of Europe, except perhaps the Balkans, but I doubt this book has ever been in such a terrifying places. If it had, it would have been burnt for kindling. Those people are known for slitting throats, not collecting the rare books."

"What about France?" asked Baker. "The French adore Carroll and there are large collections there."

"The French only seriously collect the French editions. To them, all others are inferior. Perhaps they are correct. Many French collectors are my customers and I have asked them myself. They know nothing. *Absolument rien!*"

He handed Baker another letter. "This one is from Alan Tannenbaum. There isn't a Carrollian alive in North America that he doesn't know. Again, nothing! *Nichts!* I'm thinking that takes care of this continent, including Canada, though I admit that I'm not sure about Mexico. Do you know if Tannenbaum has any contacts in Mexico?"

"I have no idea, but it wouldn't surprise me. I know that he has an extensive collection of Mexican comic books and Spanish editions of *Alicia*."

"That is interesting. I didn't know that. Perhaps I have something for him. I will contact him. And finally, this letter is from the pre-eminent Japanese collector, Momma-san. Still again, nothing. That pretty much takes care of Asia. I suppose that he's got copies of every Japanese, Chinese, and Indian edition of *Alice* ever printed. So, basically, nobody knows anything in the entire civilized world. Well, I suppose there might be some collector on another planet who has seen it, but sadly, I don't know any aliens to ask them!"

Baker laughed. "What about South America, Australia, New Zealand, Africa, and Antarctica?"

Hutmacher's expression drooped. "You are right," said Baker. "I don't know anybody in those far-off places to ask either. I admit that a few of them are at least partially civilized. Do you think that they collect Carroll books? I'm pretty sure that the penguins don't, so maybe we can ignore Antarctica. I'm sure that some Australians, a Mr Howick, I have heard of, and New Zealanders collect them; maybe even an Argentinean or two. I think you've done your homework for most of the likely possibilities." He handed the letters back to Hutmacher. "So, how did you acquire the book?"

"I bought it from the widow of its last owner, a despicable man named Huey P. Rowlands of Selma, Alabama. He was a white supremacist, who went to jail for some civil rights violations. As fate would have it, he was murdered by a young white woman, who stabbed him in the eye with an ice pick one night in 1956 in the Southern Pride Bar." He handed Baker a photocopy of a newspaper clipping about the incident. "Who says that there is no justice in the world?"

Baker read it. "Ouch!" he said. "It penetrated right into his brain! It reminds me of the way they used to perform lobotomies."

"Yes. This is how my nervous wife's surgery was done. It was a miracle. It calmed her down. Now she is dead—rest her soul. Mrs Rowlands wasn't sure how her husband acquired the book, though she thought that he had got it from a war veteran, who brought it back with him from Europe. I have no idea how it got from Samoa to Europe."

"Can you provide me with Mrs Rowland's address or phone number so that I can contact her for verification?"

"I have the phone number, but it would do you no good."

"Why not?"

"Tragically, she too is dead."

"Really? When did that happen?"

"About a month ago. An automobile accident." He leafed through the folder and produced a photocopy of a newspaper clipping, which he handed to Baker. "Here are the details."

Baker scanned the short clipping, which described a horrific head-on collision when a jackknifing tractor-trailer came across the median. Her car had burst into flames on impact. Baker handed it back to him and changed the subject. "One ruby is missing. For the price you are asking I think you should replace it."

"I could have easily had it replaced. Rubies are cheap! But I have not tampered with the book. I never do such a thing with a rare book. I leave such decisions up to the buyer. In my view, the missing ruby adds to the book's mystique. One naturally wonders what might have happened to cause its loss. You can see that the setting is crushed, so perhaps it was struck by something."

"Like a rifle butt or the heel of a jackboot?"

"Perhaps. Who can say?"

"Or perhaps by a hammer wielded by a book dealer?" Baker asked, grinning like a sarcastic Cheshire-Cat.

"Are you accusing me?"

"No, I was just joking."

"It was not so funny."

"Sorry. How much did you pay for the book?"

"That is my secret, which I will take with me to the grave. Let me just say that Mrs Rowlands did not recognize the book's true value."

"And you didn't tell her."

"Of course not. I am in business. I am not the *Antiques Roadshow*."

"Will you take ten?"

"No. It is out of the question. If you are not interested, I will next offer it next to Mrs Muldoone."

"I really doubt that a woman is going to be interested. The binding is too masculine—and gothic."

"You might find surprises lurking. For Mrs Muldoone money is only a minor concern. I am sure that she would simply sneeze at twenty thousand dollars for something so rare and special as this book. But if she does not want the book, then someone else will. For instance, Marilyn Manson is a Carroll enthusiast and will soon star in a version of *Alice*. I suspect that she would like to own this book."

Baker's eyebrows went up. "Manson isn't a woman," he corrected.

"Are you sure?"

"Yes," he said. "It's a stage persona. I heard that his project had been cancelled, though."

"That is a pity. I have always thought of her as quite attractive—in a strange sort of way, of course. She would make the wonderful Alice."

"Or Duchess, with all that make-up," Baker suggested as he handed the book back to him.

"That too. So, what is your decision?"

"Give me twenty-four hours to think it over."

"Of course," Hutmacher replied, shrugging as he returned the book to the case, along with the thick correspondence file. "You may leave me a voice mail message. I will hold it for one week." He handed him a business card. "Here is my number."

"What is your e-mail address?"

"I have none. I hate computers! They are evil. I think they hate me as well! They never do what I want them to do."

Quite inexplicably, Baker suddenly felt the hair on the back of his neck stand on end and he had the very strong impression that someone was staring at his back. He wheeled around, but saw no one. When he turned back to Hutmacher he was surprised to see him standing and staring at something behind where Baker was sitting, his face blanched.

Baker involuntarily jumped when Hutmacher screamed. He was waving his hands in front of his face, as if trying to fend off a swarm of invisible bees. He then suddenly clutched at his chest, gasped and collapsed, missing his chair and landing heavily onto the floor. Baker turned slowly, looking completely around the room, but still saw nothing. Then he noticed that the tingling sensation on the back of his neck had gone, as if whomever it was that had been in the room had left.

He rushed around the desk to check Hutmacher's pulse, and couldn't find one. He stood up and reached for the phone to dial 9-1-1, then realized that if he wanted the *Snark* he would have to seize the moment. If Hutmacher died everything in the room, including *Feeding the Boojum*, would almost certainly be sold at auction or be given to some university's special collections.

He decided to wait five minutes to place the call; just to be sure that Hutmacher wouldn't make a miraculous recovery. While he was waiting he opened the Solander case and dumped his wallet, airplane tickets and keys inside, and then closed it.

After five minutes he checked Hutmacher's pulse again to be sure he was still dead and then called 9-1-1, pretending to frantically report a heart attack and giving instructions where he was, knowing that the message would be recorded. He went to the front door and unlocked the deadbolts and propped the door open with a chair. He then went down to the entryway to let the paramedics in when they arrived.

The paramedics came rushing inside about five minutes later. It only took one of them a few seconds to determine that Hutmacher had no pulse. They worked on him feverishly for ten minutes, to no avail. One of the paramedics finally placed a call to the police and requested a coroner.

About fifteen minutes later a detective came in and after talking briefly with one of the paramedics walked over to Baker. "Detective Poole. Homicide," he said "And you are?"

"Thomas Baker."

"Can I see some identification, please?"

Baker casually opened the Solander case and removed his Massachusetts driver's licence from his wallet, making no effort to hide the *Snark*. He handed the licence to Detective Poole, who copied down the details in a pocket notebook. "Were you with the deceased when he suffered his attack?"

"Yes. We were in the middle of a conversation discussing the value of a book when he suddenly stood up, screamed, grabbed his chest, and then collapsed. He fell hard. I wouldn't be surprised if he shattered his pelvis. I'm the one who called 9-1-1."

"Why didn't you perform CPR on him?"

"I was afraid that I might break his ribs or crack his sternum; even puncture a lung. He is very old—83—and fragile. He had emphysema."

"How do you know these things about him?"

"He told me. We were talking about taking a trip to Samoa, and he explained that he had always wanted to visit there, but he was too old and too sick now."

"It would have been better to break a few of his ribs trying to save him than to just let him die."

"I didn't want the liability."

"There are good Samaritan laws. You wouldn't have been charged and he wouldn't have prevailed in a lawsuit even if you had."

"I didn't know that. I'm not from here."

"What brings you to New York, Mr Baker?"

"Business. I have meetings with IBM starting tomorrow. I took the opportunity to drop by and see Mr Hutmacher. We had an appointment at 10:00 this morning."

Detective Poole walked over and looked at the desk calendar. "Yes, I see that he has you noted for 10:00. Is that your case?" he asked, pointing to the Solander.

"Yes."

"Do you mind if I have a look inside?'

"Of course not." Baker pushed the still-opened case over to him. Poole rifled through it.

"Is this the book you were discussing?" he asked, holding up *Feeding the Boojum.*

"Yes. I brought it along so that Mr Hutmacher could appraise it."

He thumbed through it, bending a few pages. Baker cringed, but held his tongue. "So what did he tell you?'

"Only three hundred dollars."

"*Only* three hundred?"

"Yes. As you can see, it's in poor condition."

"That's a heck of a lot to pay for a beat-up old book of poetry!"

"I'm sure that most people would agree with you."

The detective put it back in the case, snapped the lid shut and handed it back to Baker. "Thanks for your co-operation, Mr Baker. Where are you staying while you're in New York City?"

"At the Helmsley Park Lane."

"All right. You can leave. If we need to get in touch with you I have your address. I doubt that will be necessary; pending the results in the autopsy report, of course. You didn't kill him, did you?"

This caught Baker off guard. "Are you serious?"

"Of course; I'm always serious when dealing with a corpse— especially a wealthy one." Poole studied him as he responded, to see if his body language hinted that he was lying.

"No, I didn't kill him. We were just talking when he suddenly had his attack. I assume it was his heart."

Poole concluded that he was probably telling the truth. "That's my assumption, too. I just wanted to hear what you had to say—for the record."

Nervously, Baker returned to The Helmsley Park Lane and went straight into the elegant bar and ordered a stiff drink.

At the same time that Baker was downing a double-scotch, Detective Poole rushed out into the busy street, intent on hurrying over to his squad car that was parked on the opposite side of the road. He glanced left, but his vision was obscured by a thick cloud of smoke, which he mistook for diesel exhaust, and failed to see the fast-moving taxi until it suddenly emerged through the dense haze. It was too late for either him to jump out of the way or for the screeching taxi to stop in time. The impact knocked him twenty feet through the air, shattering his left leg below the knee where the bumper struck him. He slid to an abrupt stop against a curb, bumping his head and knocking himself unconscious. After five hours of emergency surgery it appeared that he would probably survive, but his tennis days were definitely over.

Back in the bar, Baker had sat the case on top of the table and opened it to look at what he had stolen. His adrenaline was still elevated from the thrill of committing what he believed to be a perfect crime. He picked up the *Snark* and looked at the cover, moving it back and forth slightly so that the ruby caught the light from a pencil-spot directly overhead. He flipped over to the map and studied it a moment. He decided then and there to arrange a trip to American Samoa.

"Who knows," he thought, "I might even meet a boojum on Olosega!" In the alcoholic haze he felt from having downed two quick doubles, this struck him as a very funny possibility and he laughed out loud.

A hungry light glimmered in the ruby eye.

AUTHOR'S NOTE

I have played a little fast and loose with history, which records that Robert Louis Stevenson actually died on the *morning* of December 3, 1894. Many years later his house was badly damaged by a typhoon, but it has now been restored as a museum in his memory, though the only original furnishings to be seen there are three chairs. Stevenson was never definitively diagnosed with tuberculosis, though it is generally believed that he suffered from this disease, which was largely responsible for his having moved to Samoa, where he was able to breathe with less discomfort.

Other than Stevenson, his wife, and a few modern-day Carrollians, all characters in this story are fictional.

I have no idea if Stevenson actually owned a copy of *The Hunting of the Snark*, though it is not difficult to imagine that he might have or that he would have at least read it.

Moas are quite real. In 2002 the *Samoa Times*, an online newspaper, reported that they were believed responsible for the mysterious disappearances of ten badly-behaved children on Olosega alone.

(Okay. I made that part up.)

The West Virginia Snark
Hunting Society

The West Virginia Snark Hunting Society
Five miles north of Tad on Big Bottom Road (County Route 48)

To the Highly Esteemed: *Maker of Bonnets and Hoods*

Your presence is required at Boojum Hall on Friday, May 13th
at 5:00 p.m. precisely for the Society's Annual Meeting.
Barbecue and beer will be available.
Formal attire required.

This year's guest Snark will be Bryon Swell who will speak
on a topic of great interest to all: *Deer Season Angst.*

Don't bother with a RSVP. Just be there.
The Bellman

The West Virginia Snark
Hunting Society

*E*van's invitation to the 2011 West Virginia Snark Hunting Society's Annual Meeting arrived in his mailbox out by the road on May 13. He studied the postmark to be sure that it had been hand stamped on May 10 as required by the Society's bylaws, which stipulated that it was to be posted on the Tuesday immediately prior to the first Friday the 13th of the year, unless there wasn't one that year, in which case it was to be posted on the third Thursday of January. Since he was a snark collector, he took the invitation inside to the kitchen table and got a paring knife to carefully slit the envelope open without doing any serious damage to either the envelope or its contents.

The RSVP note was no tongue-in-cheek joke or idle threat, and members took it very seriously, for good reason. Only one excuse was acceptable: incarceration, this considered to be well beyond the crewmember's control, even if he did get caught, as long as he had vigorously resisted arrest. There were two former members who had foolishly missed an Annual Meeting. Both had been discovered dead during the following deer hunting season. One, the acting Beaver, had presumably fallen from his tree stand (Ha!), a distance of about twenty-feet, in 1956. The other, the acting Barrister, had been discovered during bow season in 1973 with an arrow protruding from the back of his camouflage hunting jacket. Both deaths were considered suspicious by the West Virginia State Police and were treated as cold cases. Crewmembers had at various times missed the birth of a son or daughter (four times), their own wife's funeral (once), their own wedding (twice), and one Butcher had even given away tickets to Super Bowl XXV, though this had been almost impossible to comprehend. One crewmember on hearing this had remarked that "I personally would have gone to see the game and then faced the music." So if a crewman knew that if for some reason he was going to have to unavoidably miss an Annual Meeting then he had little choice but to resign. Naturally, resignation was considered an act of supreme cowardice by the other crewmen, who would thereafter shun him and even refuse to attend his funeral.

Not too surprisingly, all past and present members of the Society were good ol' boys. No women were ever invited, because the Invitation Committee fully realized that none were at all likely to accept, since they invariably hated it when men ate with their hats on (usually backwards to avoid getting gravy on the bill), and that they didn't want to have to constrain themselves from belching or cursing if a woman happened to be present. And it wasn't that they were racists either. There was no rule against asking a foreigner or other non-white human to join. In fact, to prove the point, they had once actually invited a Japanese assembly line worker from over at the Toyota plant in Buffalo, West Virginia, to join, but (for some reason they could not fathom) he had declined. His lame excuse had been that he really didn't like slaughtering wild animals, even if they were considered edible or an invasive species, and that he didn't care for the taste of raccoon or possum, even if served as sushi on a bed of Uncle Ben's instant white rice. The worker had inexplicably returned to Hokkaido a week later.

When Evan had joined he had at first been embarrassed to learn that he would be the Maker of Bonnets and Hoods, since it sounded so sissified and everything. But his initial reaction was soon mollified when he understood that it simply referred to hunting caps and baseball hats, of which all members owned at least a dozen examples. So, once this had been explained he carried the title with manly pride and took it upon himself to provide, at his own considerable expense, each crewmember with a new neon-orange hunting cap at the beginning of deer hunting season. This gesture was naturally greatly appreciated and it was maintained by all that it was likely the reason that no one in the Society had ever been shot in the head, whether in a deer stand, at the dinner table,or in a restaurant—since they almost never take them off.

Evan drove his pickup onto the lawn of Boojum Hall, an old farmhouse that the Society had purchased many years ago, along with the 3,000 acres of woods and fields that surrounded it. The crewmembers had spent two weeks converting it into the Hall. When they were finished there were ten bunk beds, a very large kitchen with four mismatched refrigerators for beer on one wall and two huge top loading freezers on the other for the meat of various species. There were two bathrooms with wall urinals, toilets, and a small shower stall (cleanliness not being a very high priority to most of them). There was also a large room that served as their meeting room. It normally had two pool tables set up. These were pushed back out of the way once a year for the Annual Meeting. They had also meticulously posted the entire perimeter of the property with NO HUNTING signs in a vain attempt to keep the deer for themselves. It was impossible to enforce on such a large place, and they were constantly rushing out during deer season to fire warning shots at the neighbors or out-of-staters who snuck in on the property to shoot one of their famous big bucks.

There were already eight pickups on the lawn, most having arrived much earlier, when Evan had driven up. He went on into the Hall and found Darryl Frickey and Lawrence Looby playing eight-ball. "Hey Darryl! Lawrence! How you guys doin?"

"Fine," Darryl said.

"Fine," Lawrence echoed. "You?"

"Fine," Evan said. "Whar's the others?"

"Out back," Darryl said, "grillin some venison steaks. You ought go tell em iffen you want one, so they're sure to be enough for you."

"Okay. Thanks. I'll jest do that."

Evan went out back and immediately noticed that there was some idiot standing in the smoke next to the propane grill dressed up in a tux. He walked over to him and extended his hand to shake. "I'm Evan," he told the stranger. "Who the hell are you?"

"I'm the Snark," Bryon replied. "My alias is Bryon Swell."

"Why're you in a monkey suit? You goin to a funeral or somethin after the meetin?"

"No. The invitation said formal attire was required."

Evan laughed. "You mean no one tole you that meant to show up in clean camos?"

"No," Bryon said. "I wish they had. I'm going to have to pay to have this thing dry-cleaned now that it smells like mesquite smoke and burned deer meat."

Evan laughed again. "I think you're the first guy what ever showed up to one of these meetins in a tux!" He laughed again.

"If I had shown up in camouflage and the rest of you were in tuxedos then you probably would have tarred and feathered me."

"Nah, we couldn't'a done that. We ain't got no chickens! Otherwise we might'a." He laughed again, even harder, as he imagined what that might have been like. "Shoot, we gotta get us some dang chickens just in case we need em sometime! I'm goin to mention that to the Bellman!"

"You want a steak, Evan?"

"Yeah, sure, Eldon."

"Go back in an git one you like out of the green fridge an bring it out here."

"Nice to meet you, Snark," Evan sniggered and then went back in to fetch some meat.

"Evan's a good guy," Eldon said. "He just likes to poke at people; see if he can git a rise out of em."

"So, Eldon, which crewman are you?" Bryon asked.

"I'm the Baker, but I can only bake barbecue, as you can see. When I joined up I didn't understand that I'd be spendin most of my time slavin over a hot grill. But I don't really mind none. I have a good time up here."

"Doesn't it make you a bit nervous to be the Baker?"

"Why would it?"

"The Baker is the one that meets a Boojum and vanishes."

"I try not think about that. So far, so good."

Evan soon returned with a big steak on a paper plate. "Here you go, Eldon. Slap some sauce on this mama. I like it medium rare."

"I remember," he said.

"Good man!" Evan replied and whomped him on the back. He turned to Bryon. "I read on the invite that you're talkin about *angst* tonight. I was wonderin what that is, exactly."

"Dread and apprehension," Bryon replied.

"Now that's a real happy thing to talk about! Why don't you talk about somethin happy?"

"Well, this is a snark hunting society, so angst is a natural theme."

"Yeah, I suppose," Evan allowed. "Shoot, I'm sufferin some angst, now that I think about it!"

"About what?"

"I'm gettin pretty angsty about maybe Eldon here's burnin my steak!"

Eldon laughed. "I ain't burnin it!" He held it up with a long pair of thongs. "Shoot! There's still blood drippin out of it!"

"Well, put it back on my plate then, before you burn it!"

"How's this for yours, Bryon?" Eldon asked, holding his steak up for view.

"Put it back on the grill, please. I like it well done," Bryon replied.

"You mean to tell me you like it burnt?"

"No, not burnt; just no blood dripping out of it."

"That ain't blood! It's juices."

"Anyway, give it another three or four minutes, please."

Eldon looked up, "Here comes the Bellman," he said. "You want another steak, Jack?"

"No thanks, Eldon. I just came out to check on this snarky little penguin." He turned to Bryon. "You git anythin to eat yet, Snark?"

"Not yet. I'm waiting for the blood to clot up. Eldon's working on it."

"We'll be startin the meetin in about thirty minutes. Are you ready for your talk?"

"I think so. I suppose that I'm as ready as I will get."

"Good!" The Bellman walked off.

"I notice that the Bellman's the only one wearing blue camouflage," Bryon said to Eldon. "I've never seen blue camo before."

"Yeah, the Bellman wears blue. It's symbolic for being a sailor. He bought it from Navy surplus. I think maybe Seals wear it."

Bryon took his carbonized steak over to a picnic table and ate a few of the bits that weren't too black, then got up and went back into the big meeting room to collect his thoughts for a few minutes. He noticed that there was a large archery target in the shape of a bear tacked to the wall at the front. Someone had taken a Sharpie and scrawled "BOOJUM" above it in big capital letters. Around the room hung what looked like perhaps thirty white-tail buck head mounts of all sizes. Some of them had huge 12- or 14-point racks. Others were much smaller 2- or 4-point bucks. Over the doorway at the front entrance was a mounted black bear's head, with his mouth wide open in a perpetual silent roar. Bryon noticed that it had very impressive teeth.

Eventually everyone came into the meeting room and took a chair. There was much scraping of chair legs and repositioning before things finally settled down, at which point the Bellman rang a big cowbell three times. It was a deafening racket. Then he yelled at the top of his naturally loud voice, "This here 2011 Meeting of the West Virginia Snark Hunting Society is hereby called to order! Just in case you've forgotten the rules, you must refer to each other by your crew names while the meeting's in progress." He reached down and picked up a one-gallon can and slammed it down on top of the little table that he was standing next to. "If you screw up, you must put a dollar bill in this bucket. Every time! No excuses. If you didn't bring any cash then there is a pad and a pencil inside the can. You can write an I.O.U. Whatever we collect in this manner will be placed in the beer fund for the 2012 meeting. Okay, now that we got that said, let's git on with the reading of the poem. Fit the First will be read by the Boots. Come on up here, Boots!"

The Boots got up and walked to the front while the others clapped and hooted. He began in a tremulous tone:

"Just the place for a snark!" the Bellman cried
As he landed his crew with care—"

The reading of the poem went on in this manner, with each crewman reading his assigned Fit, until it was finally done. It had taken about 30 minutes. At this point there had been a wild cheer from the crew. The Bellman then declared, "Well done, mates! I know that this has made you all very thirsty, so it's time for some grog! It's time for some grog! It's time for some grog! What I tell you three times is true!"

The Baker jumped to his feet and went to get two buckets of iced long-necks, which he quickly distributed to the crew.

So far, no one had slipped up and called anyone by his real name. The painful thought of putting dollars in a bucket helped them keep their focus.

Once everyone had taken a few swigs of their beer, the Bellman stood back up. This time he had a large caliber pistol in his hand. Bryon got worried at the idea of a guy having had a few beers waving around a pistol.

Without even saying a word the Bellman turned around and taking aim, emptied six rounds into the bear target. A huge roar of approval went up from everyone except Bryon, who was speechless. It took a few moments for the smoke to clear.

Boojum

The Beaver ran up to the target and counted the bullet holes. "Six direct hits!" he declared. Again a loud cheer went up from the crew, who began chanting: "More beer! More beer! More beer!"

The Baker scurried back into the kitchen and returned with two more buckets of beer, to more applause.

The Bellman waited a few minutes and then rang his cowbell three times again. "Okay. It's time for the Snark's speech!" he declared.

This was followed by a cry in unison from the crew: "Speech! Speech! Speech!"

Bryon stood up and rather reluctantly walked up next to the Bellman, who was busily reloading his big pistol. Once he had the thing reloaded he raised his hand to silence the crowd. "For those who may not know too much about this particular little puny-looking Snark, I will tell you something about him. I won't say his real name, since I don't want to put money in the bucket. He lives in Hurricane. That's over near Teas Valley, as you may know. He has a strange hobby that we can all appreciate in a girly sort of way. He collects books instead of deer trophies."

This news was followed by a great deal of whistling and cat-calling, which the Snark did not find at all comforting.

"For some reason he likes to dress up like he's going to the opera, which is a bit girlish as well, in my opinion—" (more whistles) "—but I for one am willin to overlook these faults since the books that he collects are rare editions of *The Hunting of the Snark*."

Here a great cheer went up from the crew. Bryon was then able to breathe a bit easier.

"Personally, I'm just relieved that at least he doesn't collect Winnie-the-Pooh books! He has promised to talk with us about angst and deer hunting." He turned to Bryon and pointed the loaded pistol at his head. "Now listen, Snark, I just hope that you'll be able to make it interestin. By that, I mean that it had better not take more than about five minutes; six minutes, tops." He reached into the bucket and produced an old alarm clock, which he wound slowly. "Right, now it says 7:03. I'd strongly encourage you to be done when the little hand is on the seven and the big hand is on the nine." Having said this, the Bellman walked over and sat down with the pistol in his lap at the ready. "You best start now, Snark!" the Bellman said and gave a little wave with the pistol.

Bryon started talking as fast as he could. "Good evening. It's a pleasure to be here. I am going to talk briefly—very briefly—about Deer Season angst, which is a perfect metaphor for the meaning of the poem, *The Hunting of the Snark*. You might well want to know what 'angst' is. After all, it's not a word you hear a lot when you're in the bar with your buddies. I'm sure that you have all experienced it. You get invited to go hunt with some guy who owns a farm that's practically infested with huge bucks, as if it is a deer plague. When you get there you find out that he's brought along his seven-year old daughter, and this is the first time that she has ever gone hunting. She's armed with an expensive-looking little rifle with a big scope. In your heart of hearts you just somehow know that she's going to manage to kill an 18-point buck that will score a new Boone and Crockett record for West Virginia of at least 200. You, however, also somehow know down deep in your spirit that you will only manage to mistakenly shoot a spike buck that somehow jumps in the way of your perfect shot at a 14-pointer that gets away. You will suffer the shame and humiliation of having to put your deer-tag on the yearling, and she will get to put her deer-tag on the King of the Forest. That deep down, horrible feeling in the pit of your stomach is pure angst.

"That's what Lewis Carroll's poem is all about. The crew goes out to bag a Boone-and-Crockett-record snark. They know that there is at least a remote chance that they might encounter a Boojum, at which point it will get to hang its human-tag on one of their ears and that that crewman will vanish—or worse. It will likely eat him.

"So, now you know the point of the whole poem. In summary it means this. One: Don't go hunting with little girls. They will whip your butt every time. Two: Be sure you have a clear shot and there aren't any yearlings bounding around the meadow like stupid Bambi. What I tell you three times is true, but I don't have time to repeat what I just said two more times, because my time is up."

There was wild applause from the entire crew except for the Bellman, who was still armed and angry looking. He got up and walked slowly over to Bryon. "I am *very* disappointed that you finished in time," he told him.

"But why?" Bryon asked, in a very tremulous tone. "That's all I could manage to say in the allotted time."

"Because if you hadn't finished in time then I would have got to stand you up there in front of that Boojum target and had the pleasure of blowing you away! I'm thinking I might just do it anyway!"

Bryon fainted.

The Baker came over and dumped the ice out of one of the beer buckets onto Bryon's head, which had the effect of bringing him to. When he opened his eyes all he saw was the Baker holding an empty bucket and the Bellman holding a big pistol in his face, looking exactly like Dirty Harry. He screamed like a girl, which brought a huge round of laughter and applause from the crew.

The Bellman reached down and scraped the ice cubes off of Bryon's tuxedo. "I wasn't really going to shoot you," he said. "It was just all a joke. The Bonnet captured it all on his phone. He plans on putting it on YouTube. You can watch it when you get home tonight."

BRYON "SNARK" SWELL, FOUND MURDERED

Charleston (AP)—Kanawha Co. Sheriff Mike Rutherford has announced that the body of Bryon Swell, local restaurateur, prominent WV Lewis Carroll collector, and avid Snark enthusiast, has been recovered from a septic tank near Tad after an intensive five-day search. The body was discovered by Zeus, the Kanawha Co. Search and Rescue Team's famous mastiff cadaver dog.

"Mr. Swell was brutally murdered," Sheriff Rutherford explained during a hastily called 3:00 p.m. press conference, "as evidenced by the fact that ten arrow shafts were visibly protruding from various parts of Swell's corpse. He looked like a dang porky-pine! We believe the killer or killers had to break the arrow shafts off in order to stuff him through the septic tank manhole. Once his filthy hunting camos were removed and he had been hosed off it was noted that the word "BOOJUM" had been scrawled across his chest with an indelible black marker."

Swell's body was discovered this morning on the property of the West Virginia Snark Hunting Society (WVSHS), a secretive organization headquartered in an old farmhouse on an extensive acreage a few miles north of Tad, just off of Big Bottom Road (County Route 48, near Mill Creek). Two senior Sheriff's Department homicide detectives are presently interviewing the WVSHS's ten present members. Their leader, Jack "The Bellman" Possumback of Chelyan, reputedly a former Exalted Cyclops of a small local chapter of the KKK, has been designated a "person of interest," but has not yet been charged.

Swell, age 42, was not a member of the WVSHS, but was famously known to have been a guest speaker at the Snark Society's annual meeting held on Friday the 13th this past May. His humorous speech, on "deer hunting angst", was recorded by an unidentified Society member using his cellphone and posted on YouTube the following day. This popular online video has gone viral and there have been over 1.7 million hits to date. It shows the terrified Swell, oddly dressed in a tuxedo, giving a brief speech and then fainting when he believes that he is about to be shot point blank by Jack Possumback.

Following his famous speech, Swell took advantage of his sudden fame and opened the highly successful Snark Shack Bar and Grill located in the Teas Valley restaurant district, in the old Blockbuster Video store, which he renovated extensively. The restaurant's eclectic menu features blistering hot "Boojum Wings", "Custer's Last Sandwich", made from lean bison meat imported packed in dry ice from Montana, generous slices of "Aunt Vicki's Un-birthday Cake", and a large selection of imported beers. Swell lived alone in a small house with his beloved collection of Lewis Carroll books and his bizarre pet dog, a Chihuahua–Doberman pincer mix, ironically named "Boojum".

Bryon "Snark" Swell wearing the traditional WVSHS regalia
on the occasion of his induction into the Society

This reporter has managed to interview a former member of the WVSHS, who wishes to remain anonymous out of fear of reprisals. When asked if he had any idea who might have wanted Swell dead he replied, "He probably made some serious enemies in the Society when he recently published his little exposé about them. Bad things usually happen to people who break the Society's strict Code of Silence or other rules." When asked if there were members who were bow hunters he said that "everyone in the Society is an expert bowman."

Funeral arrangements have been postponed pending the completion of an autopsy, even though the cause of death seems relatively obvious.

—Dastárd Spewingfield

Polka-dot Snark

Polka-dot Snark

I

$\mathcal{K}$anawha County Deputy Sheriff Robert Bibbee pulled into the employee parking lot at DuPont's Belle chemical processing plant, situated on the banks of the Kanawha River a few miles east of Charleston, West Virginia, and made his way over to the guard shack at the employee entrance gate. He got out and spoke to the security guard on duty. "We got a call about somebody's vehicle gettin keyed. You know anything about that?"

"Yeah. It was Forrest Coffman's vehicle. He's over there at the other end of the lot," he said, pointing in that direction. "He's wearin a yellow hard hat. I think he's waitin on you."

Deputy Bibbee turned and looked. "Yeah, I see him. Thanks." He drove over to where Coffman was standing and got out. "I'm Deputy Bobby Bibbee. I understand you've had your vehicle vandalized."

Forrest shook hands with Deputy Bibbee. "Come over here to the driver's side and I'll show you the damage."

Deputy Bibbee studied the door panel. "This don't look like no key job, Mr. Coffman—way too neat. Whoever done this didn't just scratch your SUV and walk away. My guess is they took their time and done it with some sort of tool, like a ice pick, maybe. S–N–A–R–K. Mean anything to you?"

"No."

"What about this little pitchure below the writin. Thet looks like some sort of animal. You know what thet is?"

"It looks like a child drew it. My guess is it's supposed to be a beaver. Big buck teeth. Flat tail. Or could be squirrel roadkill, I suppose."

"Yeah—could be," Deputy Bibbee agreed. "Probably some kid pranked you. You got insurance?"

"Yeah, but five-hundred deductible for comprehensive."

"Ouch! You got any idea who might'a done it?" Deputy Bibbee asked.

"Not really. But if you look up there on that light pole you can see there are security cameras covering the entire lot. Whoever it was is probably on tape."

Deputy Bibbee looked up to where he was pointing. "I don't think they actually use tape anymore."

"You know what I mean. DVD or whatever. I'm the wrong generation for all that computer lingo."

"Yeah. Let's go see if we can find somebody to give us a look-see. We can drive over in my cruiser."

Back at the guard shack, Bibbee told the guard what he wanted, and the guard made a phone call. "Go on over to the Admin Building and sign in with the receptionist. She'll call Security for you." They were soon sitting in a small office watching a computer monitor playback the recording for the camera that covered the zone where Coffman had parked.

"Stop!" Deputy Bibbee said. "Now back it up just a little. Good. Now forward, real slow-like." They watched as someone clothed entirely in black and wearing a biker's helmet got off of a dirt bike and left the visor down. "Looks like a dang ninja," Bibbee remarked then laughed. Coffman didn't think it was funny. The security guard didn't say anything. The rider went around to the driver's side of Forrest's SUV and a few minutes later returned to the bike and sped away. "Can you back up and zoom in on the bike's license plate?" Deputy Bibbee requested.

The stone-faced Security Officer did, but all it revealed was an illegible plate completely covered in dried mud. "Well, thet sure ain't no help," Deputy Bibbee observed then turned to Coffman. "Sometimes you can tell who a person is just by seein how they walk. Look like anybody you recognize?"

"No. But the narrow hips make me think it might be a teenage boy. That and whoever it is, is good on the bike. Lots of practice, I'd say."

Deputy Bibbee turned to the Security Officer. "We're done, I guess. Thanks for your help." They signed out and left the building.

"You want me to drive you back to your vehicle?" Deputy Bibbee asked.

"No, thanks. I need the exercise. I'm steamed about what happened to my new SUV."

"You got any enemies what might want to damage your vehicle?"

"There's a few people who aren't exactly fond of me, but I can't think of anyone who would stoop to doing that." This was more of a lie than simple understatement.

"Maybe a co-worker here the plant, for instance?"

"No. I git along fine with everyone at the plant."

"You ever been married?"

"No."

"How about an ex-girlfriend what's angry with you then? Vandalizin a vehicle like that is usually somethin a woman might do if she's been jilted."

"No," Forrest lied again. Truth was, there was a long list of women possibilities. At the top of the list were four women, each of who was raising one of his four kids. He'd never bothered to marry any of them. He rationalized his behavior by telling himself that he was just doing his part in replenishing the earth like God had instructed Noah to do; not that he really believed there ever was a Noah—or a flood. This was one of the few Biblical injunctions he had managed to keep, though.

"Well, if someone eventually comes to mind, give me a call. I'll go talk to them."

"I will. Thanks for coming out."

"No problem. I'll file a report for the record in case something else happens and we need to follow up. You might want to keep your vehicle in the garage for a spell," Deputy Bibbee advised.

"Ain't got one," Forrest replied. "I live in a trailer."

"Then you might want consider gettin yourself a big mean dog."

"I got one of them already. A pit bull named Ulysses. If he doesn't know you then he's goin to try to bite you. I keep him on a very long leash. You'd have to shoot him to get near my SUV at night."

"Good."

11

Forrest was naturally depressed. He drank a large whisky and went to bed early. He slept sound and didn't hear anything unusual all night. The next morning when he went to get into his SUV to go to work he found that someone had spray painted the entire side of his SUV except the windows. The worst part of it was that they had used a Pepto-Bismol shade of pink. He cursed loudly, then touched the paint to see if it had dried. Unfortunately, it had. The empty spray can and its pink plastic cap lay on the gravel nearby. He picked up the can, hoping to see that it was latex. It wasn't. He went to the back of the car and found that someone had scratched a small beaver design on the trunk lid. It looked pretty much like the one that had been inscribed on his door panel a few weeks earlier.

He then noticed that someone had painted bright pink spots all over Ulysses. "What kind of guard dog are you?" he demanded, as if the dog could understand him. "Bad dog!" he yelled, furious with him. Ulysses tucked in his tail and slunk under the trailer where he had a bed and a place to stay out of the rain. Forrest went over to the opening and yelled at him. "From now on, I'm callin you Useless. You might as well start gittin used to it!"

Forrest stood awhile in uffish thought, looking at his now half-pink SUV and considering his ridiculous pink-spotted dog that looked like something Dr. Seuss might have dreamt up in a nightmare. He started talking out loud to himself. "Well, I assume that since Useless didn't kick up a fuss last night, and that since I don't see no blood splattered all over the gravel, whoever the jerk was what did this was somebody the dog knows real well. That would include three of the four mamas of my kids." He pondered for a moment and then continued. "I guess it's got to be Betty, Billie, or Blossom. Probably Billie. She's got a vindictive nature." He glanced down at the long scar on his left forearm where she had cut him with a butcher knife in the heat of an argument about a girl she had seen him with at a local bar. He was lucky. She had meant to slit his throat, but he blocked the blow with his left arm and it got cut instead. "I should've pressed charges on her—even if I was guilty of trying to replenish the earth without her involvement."

He briefly considered driving into work in his car painted like it was, but knew that he would never live it down. He got out his phone and called in sick. The guy he was supposed to relieve at shift change was going to be mad, since he'd have to stay over to cover for him. He called the Sheriff's office and asked for someone to come out and take a look. As it happened, Deputy Bibbee was the one dispatched on the call. When he drove up he recognized Forrest, recalling the incident in which his SUV had been vandalized. Useless went ballistic when he heard the deputy's cruiser pull onto the gravel in the drive and came charging out from under the trailer intent on ripping out the throat of whoever it was that had dared to enter his territory. Deputy Bibbee stayed in the car until Forrest could restrain the dog.

Once it was safe, Deputy Bibbee stepped out. "That's quite a dog you've got," he observed.

"Yeah, I used to think he was the perfect guard dog. Kill anything that came close to my vehicle or trailer, but I've changed his name to Useless. I'm not happy with him."

"Useless?"

"Yeah, I used to call him Ulysses, but I changed his name today. He didn't do squat about preventing what happened last night."

"Why the heck have you painted pink polka dots all over him?"

"I did'n do that! He's been decorated by The Snark. The jerk also painted the driver's side of my SUV pink."

Deputy Bibbee was unable to stifle a laugh as he looked at the dog. He walked over to examine the SUV. "Someone is sure nuff mad at you!"

"Evidently," Forrest agreed.

"It looks like you're now selling Mary Kay cosmetics!" He couldn't help laughing again. "Whoever is doin this seems to have a sense of humor."

"I ain't laughin. Maybe someday I'll look back and find it funny, but I doubt it. Right now I'd like to beat the snot out of whoever it was."

"No, I wouldn't do that. I'd have to arrest you for assault and battery. You sure you're not havin trouble with a girl-friend? Pink seems like a pretty obvious gender message!"

"Well, I've got four kids, by four different women, and every one of them women is mean. Could be one of them, I suppose. In any event, it has to be someone that Useless recognizes. Otherwise he would have tried to tear them to pieces and I would have heard the ruckus. That eliminates the first one, since she never met the dog, as far as I know."

"You paid up on child support?"

"No, I'm fallin behind," he admitted. "As it is, I can barely afford to eat. I'm just glad that I never married any of them. Alimony would be the literal end of me."

"The judge will adjust the child support for you. The court don't want you to starve to death. They realize that if you starve then you cain't pay your child support. They're not *that* stupid."

"Yeah, I know. I need to go see the judge about doin that."

"What do you want me to do?" Deputy Bibbee asked.

"I just want you to report that I've been vandalized again, in case my insurance company balks at paying to have the SUV repainted—or in case someone shoots me or somethin."

"Why'd you say that? You received any threatenin phone calls lately?"

"No more than usual. Most weeks I get two or three. Nothing serious ever comes of them, so I just ignore them. I do have a permit to carry, however; just in case."

"Can I see your permit, please?"

"Sure." He took it out of his wallet and handed it to him.

"You carryin right now?"

"Yeah." He lifted up his shirt tail to reveal a small semi-automatic pistol in a holster on is belt.

"You take it into work with you?"

"Yeah, but I lock it up in my glove compartment before I go in. They'd fire me if they caught me carryin it inside the plant. Truth is they'd probably fire me if they found it in my car if it was parked in the lot. I don't dare tell anyone about it."

"About them threatenin calls—you ought to keep a log with dates and times. They might be traceable if somethin was to happen to you. Is it men or women what call?"

"Both, but usually it's one of my ex-girlfriends that thinks I haven't been treatin her right. It's hard to please them. I usually recognize their voices, but not the men's. They're probably one of their latest boyfriends or a relative. I don't know. "

"What are they threatenin to do, exactly?"

"Oh, all sorts of things. They have scary imaginations. Some of them tell me they're going to kill my dog; some of them say they're going to burn down my trailer with me in it some night while I'm asleep. One of them keeps mentionin skinnin me alive. That sort of stuff. I just figure that they watch too many violent movies and that gives em ideas. I have this bad feeling that one of these days I'm going to have to shoot one of them, even though I really don't want to do that. Not that I'd miss em. I'd probably get arrested even if I was just defended myself and I'm not too sure how a jury would like hearin about all of my kids and stuff."

"You might want to consider movin to a different state. A different county might not be far enough."

"Nah, I'm not afraid. Besides, I like it here in West Virginia. We don't get no big tornados. No volcanos. No hurricanes. No earthquakes. Not too much snow. No forest fires that I can recall. No killer bees or twenty-foot-long rock pythons like they now have crawlin all over Florida eatin pets. The only real downside, besides the pervasive poison ivy and the occasional rabid raccoon or bat, is some of the folks what live up here in the high hollers and up on the ridges. They can get real mean if you get crossways with em."

"That's probably true about folks no matter where you live. You might want to think about gettin another dog; one that likes to bark at everything that moves."

"Shoot, I can barely afford to feed one dog, much less two! And Useless would likely just kill it and eat it anyway. He's hungry all the time."

"Is that a hunting camera you're holdin?"

"Yeah. When you drove up I was just fixin to go mount it on one of them trees over there to see if I can get a picture of whoever's doing this stuff to me."

"I've been thinkin about getting me a few of them cameras. I hunt deer and turkey over on my uncle's place in Mingo County. What kind is it?"

"It's a Primos TruthCam 35 Trail Camera, which is one of the cheapest ones."

"What's it cost?"

"Right at a hundred bucks if you buy it online."

"That's not exactly cheap."

"The more expensive ones run up to well over two hundred."

"I guess I'm goin to have to forget about thet idea. I was hopin they might just cost thirty dollars or somethin. With my luck some other hunter would probably steal it anyway." He took a notepad out of his shirt pocket. "OK, I need to know the names of all them angry women who are raisin your kids for you. Phone numbers and addresses, if you know em. We find you dead out here someday, painted pink and missin the skin off your backside, then we'll want to start our inquiries with them four."

Forrest told him what he knew. "Betty moves around a lot—from one guy to the next; every few months or so. I'm not sure if they get tired of her or if it's the other way round. I can't keep track of her. She's the oldest. She's poisoned my teenage daughter, Cassey, against me with bad talk and now the kid doesn't even want me to come by and see her. I'm not real sure where Betty's living at the moment. Last I heard she was shacked up with some guy up a high holler in Roane County."

"Does one of them seem more likely to be doin this stuff than the rest of em?"

"That would be Billie. She's been as mad as a coyote with a foot caught in trap at me for years. Billie's someone who could walk up to Useless spray paint pink polka dots all over him and survive to tell the tale. She's the alpha-dog as far as he's concerned. She could likely cut off one of his ears and he'd think that he somehow deserved it and never even growl at her as long as she rubbed his belly afterwards. She'd probably like to cut off one of my ears as well, but I'd definitely growl at her if she tried, belly rub or not."

Deputy Bibbee chuckled. "I might just drop by and pay Billie a visit," he said. "Just get to know her a bit. See how she talks about you."

"I recommend that if she invites you inside her house that you go in with your pistol drawn."

"That bad, huh?"

"Well, she might be nice to *you*—she does have a thing for big strong policemen in uniform—but I'd be on my guard, if I was you. She's a real looker and you're her type." He grinned.

"I'm a happily married man!" Deputy Bibbee protested.

"That's good," Forrest replied and grinned even bigger, "but you ain't seen Billie yet, neither."

I I I

A week later the Snark paid Forrest another nocturnal visit, this time spray painting a design of what looked like a tool shed mounted on top of wagon wheels—rather like a festive version of a Conestoga wagon. Once again the Snark's artistic medium of choice was a can of pink spray paint. It was brazenly painted on the side of the trailer directly beneath Forrest's bedroom window. Useless lived up to his new name.

Forrest phoned the Sheriff's office and asked if Deputy Bibbee could drop by and take a look; perhaps take a few photographs this time and maybe even do something high tech, like dust for a fingerprint on the spray can.

Deputy Bibbee drove up about an hour later. Useless practically exploded in a barking fit when Bibbee got out of his cruiser and walked towards the trailer. Bibbee drew his pistol just in case he had to shoot the dog. Forrest emerged from the trailer a few moments later and saw that Deputy Bibbee had pulled his gun and was pointing it at Useless.

"Don't shoot the dog!" he yelled. "I'll tie him up!" Deputy Bibbee put his pistol back in his holster and waited for Forrest to come over to where he was standing, just in case the dog got loose.

"How you been, Mr. Coffman?"

"Oh, worse that yesterday, but no doubt better than tomorrow."

Deputy Bibbee laughed. "I hear you. The Snark paid you another visit, did she?"

"Yeah. Painted a dang mural on the back side of my trailer. Come on around and I'll show you. I wish that Snark would stick to tagging box cars and leave me alone."

"Is it obscene?"

"No, just weird."

As they were making their way to the back Deputy Bibbee offered some more advice. "You might want to think about whackin these tall weeds back from your trailer. You just might step on a rattler someday comin back here iffen you don't."

"Yeah, I know. I've been meanin to do that. Just haven't gotten around to it. Rattlers don't come around here, though. I think they're afraid of Useless. You bring a camera?"

"I've got a phone."

They walked over to the vandalized portion of the trailer. "What the heck is *that* supposed to be?" Deputy Bibbee asked.

"I was hoping you might know. Looks like an outbuilding of some sort mounted on top of axels with big old pioneer style wagon wheels. It's got a long shaft that makes it look like it's supposed to be pulled by a horse. As you can see, 'SNARK-LANDIA OR BUST' has been written across the outbuilding. This is going to cost me a bundle to clean up. I might just have to leave it, since I got a big deductible on my home insurance."

Deputy Bibbee set about taking a few photos. "Let's go back around and take a few pictures of your fancy polka-dot dog as well. You hold onto him real tight, hear. I don't want to leave here in a body bag or missin a arm or a leg. I'd hate to have to shoot him, seein as you're right fond of him and everything."

"I used to be fond of him, but right now I'm not sure I would care if you shot him or not."

After taking a few photographs of a snarling pit bull, Deputy Bibbee asked, "You think you got any pictures on that huntin camera you were going to set up in them trees over there?"

"I haven't looked yet. If you got a few minutes I'll go get the disc out of it and load it into my laptop so we can take a look."

"I got time."

A few minutes later the two of them were staring intently at the laptop screen in the trailer's small kitchen area. Most of the clips were of Useless and others were of Forrest coming or going, but there was an occasional whitetail, coyote, raccoon, and possum. "Fortunately, Useless spends most of his time under the trailer and only comes out when he hears or smells something," Forrest said. "Otherwise that's all that would be on here." Suddenly a dark figure appeared on the screen. "Bingo!" Forrest exclaimed. "Here's our Snark!" A slightly built figure dressed in black and wearing a biker's helmet was handing something to the dog. "Looks like the Snark bribed Useless with a steak," Forrest observed. "Useless looks real excited to see whoever it is. His tail's a blur from waggin so hard and that's a submissive pose. That's got to be one of my ex-girlfriends or perhaps even one my kids. I don't know. Of course, it might just be one of the neighbor's teenage kids that's gotten to know him."

"What's your best guess?"

"That would still be Billie. She was the smallest one. I've never been mean to my kids—the few times I've actually seen them. Let's see if the next few clips give us a clue." He pressed forward and the screen went black. "What the heck!"

"She probably messed with your camera," Deputy Bibbee suggested.

Forrest retrieved the camera. "I didn't notice this before. The lens has been spray painted. I hope the camera's not ruined! I need this for huntin. Venison and macaroni 'n cheese is mostly what keeps me from starvin."

"From the looks of your videos you don't really need the camera. You could just set up a tree stand in your front yard and shoot as many deer or varmints as you want."

"You got a point. I might just do that. You going to dust for fingerprints now?"

"No, we just dust for prints when there's been a really serious crime, like a murder or a meth lab. The county can't afford to spend the money to check prints on silly little stuff like this. Now, if you get yourself killt then I can arrange to have a CSI Techie come out here and dust for em. We'd probably have to put your dog down first, though. There's no way a dog as vicious as he is can be adopted out to strangers."

"If I'm dead then Useless will be the least of my worries."

"Yeah. I reckon you're goin to have some serious explainin to do about all of them kids you've been dumpin across the tri-county area."

"Yeah, I reckon."

"You might want to think about a vasectomy."

"No way!"

"That's good free advice I just gave you, and you ought to take it. Anyway, I've got to get goin. I'll see if I can find your Billie and see what she has to say for herself."

I V

Deputy Bibbee located Billie Scarberry's trailer with the help of his GPS. The trailer was just off the road in a park near Frasier's Bottom, along the high bank of the river. He parked his cruiser in the street and went up and knocked on the storm door. No one answered, so he knocked again, harder this time, and yelled out "Police!" Finally, a woman opened the front door, but left the storm door closed between them. He noticed that she had a .38 in her hand, pointed at the floor.

Deputy Bibbee had to yell through the glass at her. "Are you Billie Scarberry?"

She yelled back. "Yeah. What do you want?"

"I need to talk to you about Forrest Coffman. I'd rather do that without yelling so hard that all of your neighbors can hear me." He held up his badge to the glass so that she could see it. "Please put that pistol away. I'm not going to hurt you and I don't want you accidentally shooting me with it."

She frowned and reluctantly unlatched the storm door handle. "OK. Come on in. If I decide to shoot you it won't be no accident."

She stepped back into the living room, which had all of the blinds pulled. Deputy Bibbee followed. The TV was on loud, showing an old black-and-white Cary Grant movie and provided the only light. The still air reeked of cigarettes and popcorn.

"Did you put that pistol up?" he asked.

"Yeah. I guess you'll get to live another day—if you behave yourself."

"Thank you. Would you mind turning down the TV volume? I hate having to yell at you, especially since you're obviously trigger happy."

She picked up the remote and just turned it off.

"Thank you. I'm sorry for interrupting your movie."

"It's all right. I've seen it at least twenty times and know it by heart. What is it you want to know about Forrest? I hope he's in jail or dead."

Deputy Bibbee noted that Forrest had been right about her. She was dressed in what looked like running sweats and was still beautiful. "No, he's not in jail or dead. I understand that at one time you had a relationship with Mr. Coffman."

"I guess you could call it a relationship. He got me pregnant and then abandoned me before Kyle was born. Needless to say, I am not real happy with Forrest."

"How old's Kyle?"

"Five. He's at kindergarten. Why?"

"Mr. Coffman has been having some problems with vandals."

"Good. Serves him right. Anyway, Kyle's too little to be doin stuff like that."

"Right. Anyway, vandalizing people's property is against the law and I'm trying to determine who might be doing it to see if I can get them to stop before they wind up in prison—or maybe even lose their kid."

"I'm not the one doing it!"

"I'm not saying that you are and I hope you're not. Anyway, Mr. Coffman told me that you have occasionally made threatening phone calls to him and I wanted to ask you about that."

"He's full of crap and a deadbeat dad to boot! I haven't made any threatening calls to him or anyone else. He's just a natural born liar and cheat. You can't believe a thing he says. He can look you right in the eye and tell you the biggest damn lie in the world and never blink or dilate a pupil. He should have been a poker player or an actor, and left me alone. I might have been able to marry a handsome policeman like yourself and had a happy life instead. You got a girlfriend?"

This took Deputy Bibbee aback, even though he had been warned. "I'm happily married."

A frown momentarily appeared on her face. "I'm real sad to hear that! Anyway, I didn't mean you, necessarily; just someone *like* you; big, strong, and good-lookin. I wouldn't be surprised to hear that you can even dance. Can you?"

"Yes, ma'am, I can dance a little."

"What kind? Line dancing? Ballroom? Tango?"

"You name it. When I retire I plan on opening a dance studio."

"No kidding! Whooee!"

He decided that he had better change the subject and quick. "Ms Scarberry, do you, by any chance, happen to know what a snark is?"

Billie frowned again, as if she was concentrating on a TV quiz show. "No, but it sounds like some kind of shore bird or maybe a subatomic particle. Why? Do I get a prize if I know the answer?"

He laughed. "No—sorry, no prizes. Whoever has been vandalizing Mr. Coffman's car, house, and dog has on occasion used that word."

"Vandalizing his dog? You mean Ulysses? "

"Yeah, the last time they vandalized his SUV they also spray painted pink polka dots all over him."

Billie burst out laughing. It was contagious and Deputy Bibbee couldn't help but laugh a little as well. "That dog's a real sight to see!" He pulled out his phone. "Here. I'll show you a picture of him."

Billie came over close and looked at the screen then laughed. "Now that's funny!"

"Getting back to your question," she said, still standing close to him, "I don't use the word 'snarque', since I don't speak French. Not too much use for it around here."

"French?"

"Yeah, French. S–N–A–R–Q–U–E. Snarque. Right?"

"No, ma'am, the spelling that has been used by the vandal is S–N–A–R–K."

"Really? The idiot was probably trying to spell 'shark' and was just too ignorant to know how to do it."

"I don't think so, ma'am. The perpetrator has also been leaving little drawings of a beaver; not a fish."

"A beaver? How stupid is that? That's spelled entirely different; not even close! Shoot, Kyle can spell 'beaver' better than that, and he's only five!"

Deputy Bibbee decided to drop it. "Well, I appreciate your taking time to talk with me, Ms Scarberry."

"You're welcome." She put her hand on his arm, "Hey, I just made a batch of brownies. You like brownies?"

"Yes, but I really need to get going."

"Come on. Have a brownie. I didn't put any weed in em— since they're for Kyle—and I don't have any weed at the moment anyway."

"That's very kind of you, Ms Scarberry, but I really do have to go."

"I don't normally look like I've been out jogging a marathon. Give me a minute and I'll freshen up a little, then serve you a brownie. I think I have a clean saucer somewhere. And you can call me Billie, if you like."

"Thank you, Ms Scarberry, but I wouldn't feel comfortable doing that. This isn't a social call. I'm here on official business."

"You don't like brownies, do you? How about a beer, then?" She smiled and pushed her hair back. "You like Mexican beer?

I've got a couple of Coronas? They're not too bad if you're real thirsty."

"No, thank you—really! I can't drink while I'm on duty."

"OK, I know that! I wouldn't want you to get pulled over for a DUI while you're on duty. Wouldn't be too good for your career. Well, if you ever get a hankering for a brownie you just come on back and I'll whip up a batch. Anytime; really. You know where I live now. Kyle's in kindergarten every morning till 11:30. You come early and he won't even disturb us. I won't even pull a gun on you and make you nervous."

"Thank you, Ms Scarberry. I'll keep that in mind. Look, I would appreciate it if you would let me know if you hear anything about someone vandalizing Mr. Coffman's property." He handed her a Sherriff's Department business card. He had printed his name on the back. "You can ask for me by name and I'll get back to you ASAP."

She took the card and studied it. "Robert Bibbee?" she said aloud

"Yes, ma'am. I know it's an unusual name in these parts."

"Yeah. Your name is probably unusual on the entire surface of planet Earth! Cute though."

Deputy Bibbee turned and let himself out. "Good day, Ms Scarberry. Thank you for your time."

"Please, call me Billie," she said and smiled.

He smiled back.

"Your momma call you Bobby?"

"Yes, as a matter of fact she did. Good-bye."

"Good-bye, Bobby." Then she thought, "He'll be back."

V

Two days later Forrest had an idea. He called his friend Darrell, who worked in one of the other units at the DuPont Belle plant. "Hey, Darrell! This is Forrest. Got a minute?"

"Yeah. What's up?"

"I seem to recall that you were once one of the members of the West Virginia Snark Hunting Society out past Big Bottom before it disbanded."

"Yeah, that's right. Those were the good old days."

"There's some vandals messing with my car and trailer and they keep using the word 'snark'."

"It wasn't me," Darrell said, immediately defensive.

"I know that! I didn't mean that I suspected you of any involvement. I just wanted to ask you about something."

"What's that?"

"Well, this person scratches or paints the word 'snark' on things and sometimes he or she leaves a little drawing of a beaver. That mean anything to you? I figure that you're probably a snark expert, and I don't know anybody else who is."

"That's easy, Forrest. The references are to a famous Lewis Carroll nonsense poem called *The Hunting of the Snark*. It's about a crew of ten who set out to find a mythical creature called a snark. The crewmen were all men, except for a beaver, who was the Captain's pet. You can see all of this online. Just type in the name of the poem on your search engine and you'll see all sorts of stuff about snarks and beavers."

"That's a real help, Darrell. Thanks for explaining it to me."

"You're welcome, Forrest. See you."

That evening Forrest went online and read *The Hunting of the Snark* until he came across the line about bathing machines. Not knowing what that might be he did a Google search and found a number of images of old postcards that looked a lot like what had been painted on the side of his trailer. He suddenly got the subtle message. On the way home that night he rented an 8′ × 10′ storage locker and spent the rest of the evening moving everything near and dear to him into it for safe keeping. That included his hunting trophy buck and turkey mounts, guns, ammo, night vision goggles, camping gear, four-wheeler, back issues of deer hunting magazines, and such stuff.

As it turned out, he was real glad he did. The next day he got a phone call at work. "Forrest here," he answered.

"Hey, this is Dean. You got a problem at home. I just got a call from one of your neighbors that I know and he wants me to tell you that your trailer's on fire. You might want to head on home early. See what's left."

"You joshing me, Dean? If you are, it ain't funny!"

"No, it's true. I wouldn't do that to you, Forrest."

"OK, thanks," he said and hung up. But he couldn't just rush out, since he was the shift operator and he couldn't leave until his relief showed up. And anyway, he knew that if it was true that the trailer was on fire that there wouldn't be anything left by the time he got home anyway. Trailers burn fast and furious. So, he just left at the regular time and had a beer before going home to view the charred remains.

There wasn't much left, just as he had suspected there wouldn't be. The Eleanor Volunteer firefighters had gone on home. Useless, still painted with pink polka dots, was dead. Forrest went over to see what had happened to him, hoping that he hadn't been burned, and saw that someone had shot him. It was all you could expect. The firemen couldn't fight a fire while a pit bull was trying to chew their legs off. Someone had left a note under a rock by the body: "Sorry about your dog. We didn't have a choice. He died trying to protect your trailer from us. An arson investigator will be out tomorrow about 9:00 a.m. You should meet him. It appears to us that someone burned your trailer on purpose."

He looked around for a minute to see if there was a shovel, but even that had evidently burned up, so he couldn't even bury Ulysses. He spoke out loud to the dead dog as if it could hear and understand him. "I'm not calling you Useless no more. Good boy, Ulysses! Good dog!"

He went over to the trees and retrieved the hunting camera that he had reinstalled, this time in a camouflaged location, hoping that it might have caught something that would lead him to The Snark. Then he went and bought a shovel.

V I

The first clips on the hunting camera were mostly Useless running around and barking at something, and a few more of deer and coyotes, like before. Then suddenly the volunteer firemen appeared, rushing up to fight the fire, which was already totally out of control. Fortunately, there was not a clip of someone shooting Useless. There was no sign of anyone setting the blaze. There were numerous clips of the firemen struggling to control the fire and then leaving. That was it, except for a few more clips of scavenging raccoons, a possum and a crow. He was just ready to turn off the laptop when a few final frames appeared, showing a slight figure wearing black and a biker's helmet.

"So, the Snark reveals itself once again!" Forrest said aloud. "Well, it appears that if I want to catch a wily snark I'm going to have to set a trap for it."

The next day after work Forrest stopped by the Sheriff's office and dropped off the CD of the trailer burning for Deputy Bibbee. He doubted that the deputy would see anything that he had missed, but he figured that it would be good to keep him in the loop. He went from there to the Blue and Gold Sports Bar and had a few beers while he thought about what sort of trap he might devise to catch the Snark. After pondering on it for a while a bright idea suddenly came to him.

The next day he retrieved his camouflaged tree stand from the storage unit and installed it high up in a tree that afforded a view of his burned-out trailer. Once that was in place he stocked the tree stand with bottled water, a sleeping bag, and a tight metal container with trail mix and chocolate bars inside.

The next day he went to Lowes and bought everything that he would need to build a small modern version of a Victorian bathing machine. It took him the whole day to build. When it was finished he spray-painted it white and then decorated it with big sprayed-on pink polka dots. As a final touch he wrote "SNARKLANDIA OR BUST" across the side facing the road with the pink spray paint. After that was done he covered it in a plastic tarp and went back to the motel that he was staying at and went to sleep, tired but happy.

For bait the next day he took a digital photo of the bathing machine and mailed a print of it to all three ex-girlfriends whose addresses he knew, using next-day delivery. He retrieved his night-vision goggles, deer rifle, and scope from the storage unit and returned to his place. He climbed up into his deer stand, determined to wait there for days if need be.

Two days later he heard a motorbike on the highway and he pulled up his deer rifle to scope whoever drove up. It was the same bike he had seen on the security camera at DuPont. The rider was dressed in black and wearing a helmet. The rider pulled up close to the bathing machine, got off and removed a gas can that was strapped onto the back fender, and then poured gasoline from the can onto the bathing machine. Before the rider had a chance to set it alight Forrest shot out the bike's back tire. The startled rider bolted for the highway and was soon out of sight. Forrest could have easily shot the rider, but didn't want to do that, not knowing who it was. He figured that it would be easy enough to find out now that he had the bike. As a precaution he put a second bullet through the bike's engine before he climbed down.

He walked over to the bike, now lying on its side on the gravel. This time the license plate was easy to read. He took a few photos with his phone and then called the Sherriff's office, asking for Deputy Bibbee. The deputy appeared in his cruiser about forty-five minutes later.

"What the heck is that thing?" Deputy Bibbee asked as he walked over to where Forrest was standing.

"That, Deputy Bibbee, is snark bait."

"If you say so. It looks kind of like that strange drawing the Snark painted on the side of your trailer."

"Thank you. I tried my best to make it look like it."

"Well, what is it? I still don't get it."

"That is a replica of a Victorian bathing machine. It's not exactly what one looked like. I had to use rubber tires, but it's still pretty close. Snarks are fond of bathing machines."

Deputy Bibbee looked down at the motorbike. "If you say so. I see you've killed yourself a motorbike. I wasn't aware that it was motorbike season. If you had plans to sell it then it wasn't real smart to put a bullet through the engine."

"It's not my bike, so I couldn't sell it even if I wanted to."

"Whose is it then?"

"That belongs to the Snark." Forrest took the next few minutes to explain what had happened.

"So the Snark is out there running down the highway?"

"I guess. Or perhaps hiding in the bushes. If it hadn't taken you most of an hour to get here we might have been able to find it."

"Hey, I was busy. I got here as soon as I could." Deputy Bibbee didn't feel like mentioning that he had been over at Billie's house having a brownie and a Corona when he got the call.

"I assume that it won't take too long for you to find out who owns the bike now that you have a license plate."

"Well, I can at least find out who the title is registered to. I won't know who the rider was, however." He got on the radio and called in the request to the Sherriff's office and waited. The response came back in about two minutes. "The bike's registered to a Betty Schwarz," he said. "That the Betty who was one of your old girlfriends?"

"Probably. She must have gotten married again. Last I knew she was Betty Casto."

"You think it was Betty on the bike?"

"I doubt it. She'd be too old for doing stunts like that. I feel certain it was our teenage daughter."

"That why you didn't shoot her in the leg while you had the chance?"

"Yeah. I wasn't about to shoot my own daughter, even if she did burn down my trailer and vandalize my dog."

"You want to press charges once we track her down?

"No. Just warn her to stop or next time I will. I figure I've already caused her enough grief in her young life. I don't blame her for hating me. Most women I get to know eventually do."

Deputy Bibbee suddenly turned at looked at something in the drive. "Look there!"

Forrest turned around to see what he was pointing at and saw a six-foot long rattler passing through. "Too bad Ulysses isn't around. He would have enjoyed worrying that snake."

"He probably would have got himself bit," Deputy Bibbee remarked.

"Nah, he would have probably killed and eaten it."

"So what are you going to do with your bathing machine? Thinkin about takin it down to Myrtle Beach?"

"No, I hate the beach. Since I don't need any more snark bait, and seeing as how it's all soaked in gasoline, I might just as well go ahead and watch it burn. You might want to step back a bit," he said, as he took a matchbook out of his pocket a set the entire book alight, then tossed it at a small pool of gasoline. In just a few moments the entire bathing machine was engulfed in flames.

"Too bad you don't got no beaver to barbecue," Deputy Bibbee remarked.

Dancing with Snarks

Dancing with Snarks

r Bruno Becker held up another Rorschach card. "What does this one remind you of, Herr Bieber?"

"A snark," I said without hesitation. "Just like the previous four cards."

Dr Becker dutifully recorded my response. "Most people see a vicious dog in this one. I had one patient who was reminded of his mother-in-law. You're the first one that I know of who has seen a snark. I'm curious—exactly what is a snark?"

"A snark is a fantastic creature first described by Lewis Carroll in his epic nonsense poem, *The Hunting of the Snark*. Some of them have feathers; others have scales. They're said to be very tasty, but I wouldn't know. I've never tasted one. Haven't you ever read the poem? It's famous, even in Germany."

"Yes, of course! I didn't realize that was what you were referring to. Personally, I found it depressing; too much angst."

"Some people find it humorous."

"I don't recall laughing." He held up another card. "How about this one?"

"It reminds me of the Cologne Cathedral."

"The Kölner Dom?" asked Dr Becker. "Really? Well, at least it doesn't look like a snark."

"Actually, I see a snark perched on top of the Dom roof. Right there." I pointed to it.

He held up another card. "How about this one?"

"That one looks like the Dom about 1870; before they finished the spires."

"Well, at least you don't see a snark in this one!" Dr Becker said, obviously relieved.

"Oh, but I do! It's hiding in the scaffolding. You can just see its head right there." I pointed to it.

Dr Becker turned the card around and studied it before recording my response. "You are the only person I have ever heard of who sees snarks on the roof of the Kölner Dom. Are you quite certain that you see a snark?"

"Yes; that's what I said. I say what I mean and I mean what I say."

"That sounds like something Humpty Dumpty would say."

"I suppose it does," I admitted. "It's good advice, even if it's from an egg."

"Point taken. However, most people tend to understand things within the context of what was said previously, or they try to understand things that are implied—to read between the lines. Others rely on body language or tone of voice to understand the intended meaning."

"I've never been very good at doing any of that. People need to talk plainly and truthfully if they want me to understand them," I said.

"I agree that if people would do that it would certainly make it easier to understand them. Unfortunately, that's just not how most people communicate. Those are social skills that you need to learn. I can arrange for you to have some help in that area."

"I don't want any help."

"You really need it," he assured me, then changed the subject. "So, how about this one then?" he asked, holding up yet another card.

"The Kölner Dom. This time there are two snarks on the roof."

He took a few more notes. "There are only three more cards. Please, give me your first impression, as fast as it comes to your mind." He flashed another card.

"The Dom."

He frowned. "This one?"

"The Dom."

His eyebrows arched. "This one?"

"The Dom. What I tell you three times is true!"

"I beg your pardon?" he said.

"What I tell you three times is true!"

"I believe you," he assured me, completely missing my Bellman allusion. "Were you telling the truth about the earlier cards as well?"

"Of course. I always tell the truth."

"No matter what? Even if it might hurt someone's feelings or cause a problem that could easily be avoided by just saying nothing?"

"Yes, always. If the truth hurts it's not my fault. The truth is the truth."

"So, all of the images on the cards I've just shown you remind you of either snarks or the Dom, or both?

"Yes, every one of them."

"Why are you so fascinated with the Kölner Dom?"

"I'm interested in Lewis Carroll. He visited the cathedral in 1867 on his European tour. He thought it was the most beautiful place he had ever seen. It actually made him weep when he saw it. I agree with him. It is exquisitely beautiful. Can I have the cards?"

"These cards?"

"Yes. I'd like to keep them."

"Why?"

"I collect snarks and pictures of the Kölner Dom. I'd like to have the cards for my collection."

"Yes, of course." He handed them to me. "No one has ever asked me for them before. What do you mean when you say that you collect snarks?"

"Mostly books with references to them: mysteries, science fiction and fantasy. The poem has been widely translated and illustrated by numerous artists. Plus, there is a lot of ephemeral stuff: fishing lures; model airplanes; and music, especially jazz. You can find a lot of snarks out there once you start hunting for them." I laughed and then added, "But I don't collect the real ones, of course."

"The real ones? What do you mean?"

"The creatures themselves." I paused. "But I don't tell most people I can see them. I'm only telling you, because you're my doctor and whatever I tell you is confidential. Right?"

"That's correct. I never tell anyone else anything a patient tells me unless I am consulting with another doctor or have the patient's permission. Where do you see them—the *real* snarks, I mean?"

"Oh, here and there; almost everywhere."

"Such as?"

"Well, there's one perched on the end of this couch, next to the end table. It's been listening to us, though I'm not certain that it understands German. All I've ever heard from them is squawking. They can be pretty annoying if you're trying to think or sleep."

He looked right at the snark and said, "There isn't a snark at the end of the couch, Herr Bieber."

"Can't you see it?"

"No."

I shrugged. "You're looking right at it."

"I don't see it."

"Well, it's there, whether you can see it or not. It seems to be very interested in that little vase that you have there on the end table. It'll probably break it in a moment unless you move it. Snarks are pretty destructive; they seem to like the sound of breaking glass."

He squinted, peering right at it. "Sorry, I simply can't see it. I'll just have to take your word for it, I suppose. Where else have you seen them?"

"Other than in my house?"

Dr Becker took a few notes. "Yes, other than in your house."

"I see them quite often in large stores and good restaurants."

"Why do you think that might be?"

"I assume that they like crowds. Why are you so interested in snarks, Dr Becker?"

"Actually I'm not really interested in them. I know almost nothing about them except a few lines that I can recall from Carroll's poem; something about feathers and claws—and that there's a bad kind—a boogum or a boojum, I think; something like that. I'm just interested in you, Herr Bieber. I assume that you realize that most people do not see snarks. It's a bit troubling that you do."

I nodded. "Yes, I realize that most people don't see them. It does worry me a bit."

Dr Becker nodded. "We need to figure out why you see them and if there is any way that we can make them go away."

"Oh, I don't want them to go away! I like most of the snarks I've met. It's just that I'm afraid—"

"Afraid of what?" he asked.

"A boojum," I whispered.

He stopped taking notes when I said this. "What do you think might happen if you did meet a boojum?"

"I'd vanish, of course."

"Do you mean that you might literally disappear?"

"Yes. Vanish." I snapped my fingers, startling Dr Becker, who flinched. I seemed to make him nervous.

"That won't happen," he assured me.

"It might," I argued.

"No; I'm quite positive about that. You won't disappear. I promise."

"How can you be so sure? What if you're wrong?"

"I'm not wrong. Trust me on this. That's just something you might see in a movie or read in a nonsense poem. It's not reality."

"I wish I could believe that."

"It's quite true," he assured me, then changed the subject. "Do you like to dance?"

"With you?"

"No, no! I mean with women."

"Not really. I like music, but my body has almost no sense of rhythm. I've tried. I just can't. I've even had a few lessons. It's no use."

"Do you consider yourself to be clumsy?"

"Not really. I just can't dance, but I enjoy watching other people dance. I would love to be able to dance, but I'm not one of the lucky ones who can."

"Do you have a lot of friends, Herr Bieber?"

"Do mean real friends—or just acquaintances?"

"Real ones; friends that would do almost anything for you."

"No, not many. Well, actually, none at the moment," I admitted. "I think that most people find me—well, peculiar— perhaps eccentric; I'm not sure why. I've only had a few close friends in my life." I was suddenly very suspicious about his earlier question. "Why did you want to know if I like to dance?"

"There is a possibility that you have a certain syndrome, and I—"

"What? The Two-Left-Feet Syndrome?"

Dr Becker laughed. "No, no. I believe you have several issues. Seeing snarks that no one else can see might be a bipolar condition. That can be serious. Another one is a form of autism called Asperger's Syndrome."

"So, you think that I'm autistic?"

"That's one possibility that could explain some of your symptoms."

"That's stupid! I don't see letters upside down and backwards."

"Autism comes in many different forms, with a wide variety of symptoms. Some versions are mild and people don't need any treatment at all. However, some forms are severe and can be debilitating."

"What are some of the specific symptoms you're looking for?"

"Well, some people with Asperger's are very blunt and say whatever they're thinking without considering what the impact might be. For example, a person might say, 'That's stupid!' and not realize that saying it might offend the person he's talking to."

"I just said that, didn't I?"

"Yes, you did."

"What else?"

"Well, people with Asperger's are usually not very good at small talk; they just don't see any point in it. For that reason they tend to avoid cocktail parties and many social events. They have difficulty in establishing lasting relationships or striking up a conversation with a stranger."

I thought for a moment. "That sounds like me," I admitted. "How will you confirm the diagnosis?"

"We'll just talk, like we've been doing. The more truthful you are with me, the better I will be able to confirm my suspicions."

"All right. Here's something truthful. There are actually *two* snarks in here. One is as pink as a flamingo; the other one is blue."

He turned and scanned the office. "I can't see them. How large are they?"

"Pretty big; about a meter high. These kind are harmless as long as you don't step on them. If you do that then they might bite in self-defence."

"Where do you see them?'

"The pink one is standing over there by the window, looking at the Dom. You have a nice view of it. The blue one is the one perched on top of the sofa down next to the end table. You know, you really should rescue the vase if you don't want it broken."

He obviously didn't believe me and ignored my warning. "When did you first start seeing snarks?"

"I've seen them for as long as I can remember, though I didn't have a name for them until after I had read *The Hunting of the Snark*. No one believes me when I tell them that I can see them, so I eventually quit mentioning them. Sometimes I think that I might be the only one who can see them, though I don't understand why; they're quite large and colourful. They're easy to see."

"How many snarks have you seen over the years?"

"I don't know. Hundreds, I suppose; perhaps even thousands. They're pretty common, really."

The vase on the end table suddenly went flying across the room and shattered against the wall. Dr Becker and I both flinched. "I warned you," I said.

Dr Becker tried to act like nothing unusual had happened, but I could tell that he was unnerved. "Yes, you did indeed. I should have listened to you!" He paused. "I think that will be enough for today," he said.

I nodded. "Would you like for me to chase the snarks out of here when I leave; before they break something else?"

To my surprise he said, "Yes."

"Hold the door open for me, will you?" I said as I got up. He went over and opened the door. "When I tell you to, you'll need to slam the door so that they can't run back in once I get them out." These two snarks were quick and I had a hard time chasing them out. "Now!" I yelled and Dr Becker slammed the door. "You almost slammed it on the pink one's tail!"

He shrugged. "I can't see them. Anyway, thank you, Herr Bieber, for getting them out of my office."

"You're welcome." I eased the door open just enough for me to squeeze through without letting them slip back inside. "I'll see you next week. I'm sure that the snarks will follow me out, so once I've been gone for a few minutes they won't try to get back in."

"Until next week, then," he said. He was as white as a sheet.

Close Encounters
of the Snarkian Kind

CHAPTER I

Subtle Azzigoom

"If you'll drop by my cabin in about fifteen minutes I'll show you my book collection," Captain François Boulanger suggested to Fusion Reaction Specialist Dayna Keiner. They had been talking for the last hour or so over a few too many glasses of subtle Azzigoom.

"Your book collection?"

"Yes. Old books. I haven't told anyone until now that I have them on board. I think you'd find them interesting."

"What's so interesting about some old books on a shelf?"

"Oh, I don't keep *these* books on a shelf."

"Where then?"

"In a safe."

Specialist Keiner's eyes narrowed slightly as she processed this bit of information. "Really? Now, Captain, what sort of books need to be kept in a safe? Military secrets?"

"No, no; nothing like that! Have you ever heard of Lewis Carroll?"

"Of course. Good grief! I wasn't born on Pluto! *Alice in Wonderland. Through the Looking-Glass.*"

"That's him. I have some old Lewis Carroll books."

She laughed. "I don't believe you. I'm pretty sure that they would all have been destroyed decades ago with almost every other book on planet Earth."

"Most were, but not all. I have a few. A small number of wealthy collectors also have a few. They're all quite rare, so I keep mine in a safe."

She assumed that he was lying; trying to get her alone in his cabin. However, she figured that it could be worse. He was good looking—for an old guy, anyway—and after all, he *was* the Captain. "Okay," she said. "I'll come by and take a look at your etchings."

"Books," he said. "Not etchings. Books! Look, I promise to behave myself."

"Well, if you're going to do *that*, then just forget it!"

He laughed. "My, my, my, you are quite something! But really, I have some very interesting books. You'll enjoy seeing them. I'm sure of it."

"Maybe—maybe not. Look, I need to go by own cabin and freshen up a bit first, so give me thirty minutes instead, okay?"

He nodded. "Sure. There's no hurry."

As she left the dimly lit lounge he studied her every move. She was without doubt the most beautiful woman on Mars— or any other planet or moon that he had ever visited, for that matter—she even looked great in a pink and green jumpsuit, which was saying something. The official unisex uniform was intentionally ugly, to discourage fraternization.

He told the waiter to put their "gooms" on his tab and left. It took him ten minutes to make his way through the network of corridors that ran through the *UNIS Forks and Hope*, one of a fleet of interplanetary spaceships that ferried colonizers and critical supplies from devastated Earth to Mars and beyond.

Once inside his cabin, he locked the door and went over to the wall safe, where he typed in a code and then brought his face up to the iris reader for identity verification. Moments later he heard the faint whirr of the locking mechanism.

He put on a pair of white cotton gloves before carefully removing the small stack of books that sat on top of some top-secret documents that, by interplanetary law, had to be kept in a safe. He gingerly carried the books over to the little two-person table that was welded to the floor in the center of the cabin and waited for Specialist Keiner's knock.

She was ten minutes late and he was about to give up when there was a quiet knock on the door. He opened it to find her wearing a floor-length black beaded dress with the top cut down almost to her navel and the sides slit dangerously close to her navel from the other direction. "Ah! Specialist Keiner! I had almost decided that you had changed your mind."

"Not my mind—my clothes. Sorry I'm late," she purred as she stepped inside.

"Not a problem, Specialist Keiner," he assured her.

"Please, since we're off duty, call me Dayna."

"Okay, but only if you call me François."

She smiled. "I decided to change into something a bit more appropriate for viewing your etchings, François. That uniform is hideous."

"Books, Dayna," he insisted. "Books—not etchings!"

"Yeah, right! Etchings, books; what's the difference? Anyway, I brought along a little vino that I've been keeping for just such an occasion."

"What occasion is this?"

"The one in which some handsome older man makes a move on me and asks me to drop by his cabin and look at his etchings—or stamp collection—or old books—or whatever."

This naturally encouraged the Captain, who smiled broadly. "I like your dress, Dayna—what little there is of it. Please, sit down at the table. I've put my books there." He gestured towards them.

She was genuinely surprised. "You were serious about the books!"

"Of course."

"And I thought you were just trying to lure me in here so we could be alone for games. You show me your books; I show you my—whatever."

"Well, that just might have been a secondary motive," he admitted.

"I knew it! So, here I am with a bottle of wine. Are you still intent on showing me your old books?"

"If you want to see them. I won't make you look at them if you find the idea boring."

"No, I won't be bored. It's been years since I've seen a real book that's not in a museum under lock and key!" She went over and sat down at the table, setting the wine bottle and plastic glasses on the floor, since there really wasn't enough room for them and the books too. "Why are you wearing white gloves, François? Are you worried that I might have germs or are you afraid that you might leave fingerprints?"

"No, no; nothing like that! It's because of the books. The gloves prevent further damage from the oil that's naturally on a person's hands—mine and yours." He sat down in the other chair and placed a hand on top of the books. "This is my Lewis Carroll collection. It might not look like much, but it's one of the largest, if not *the* largest, Lewis Carroll collection on Mars."

"I don't know anyone who owns a real book, much less several by Lewis Carroll!" She made a show of counting the spines, dragging the words out. "One… two… three… four… five. My word! Five!"

He smiled. "Look, I'm sure your hands are nice and clean, and I'm sorry to have to ask you to do this, but I need for you to put on a pair of these gloves before you handle the books. It's a stipulation in my insurance policy. If they check and find fresh fingerprints on them then they might well drop my coverage." He proffered the gloves.

"But I'll look ridiculous wearing those with this slinky and *very* expensive dress," she protested.

"Dayna, believe me, you could wear welder's gloves with that dress and you would still look stunning! I seriously doubt that anyone would be looking at your hands if they saw you wearing that dress."

Dayna took the gloves and smiled coyly as she slipped them on. "So you like my dress?"

"I'm a man—admittedly old enough to be your father, but I'm not dead yet. It's the stuff that dreams are made of."

"I'll take that as a 'yes'. I was just kidding about the gloves. I really don't mind putting them on, and I like Lewis Carroll. I mean, who doesn't? But I only know him from my eBook reader. It's actually very exciting to see real books! You were right. Thank you *so* much for letting me see them."

He smiled. "There's simply nothing quite like the feel of an old book," he said as he picked up the little one on top of the stack. "This," he said, beaming as brightly as a youth holding the severed head of a Jabberwock, "is the only known surviving copy of the 1968 Insel Verlag edition of *Die Jagd nach dem Schnark*. It's inscribed by the famous German bibliographer, Alise Wagner to her friend and co-editor, Udo Pasterny. They compiled a legendary bibliography called, logically enough, *The German Alice*. Unfortunately, no original copies seem to have survived. There are scans of it—so it wasn't a complete wasted effort. However, the frustrating thing is that almost nothing in the bibliography exists, as far as anyone knows. I'm only aware of six German Carroll editions: two are paperback reprintings with Tenniel's illustrations, published in the 1980s; two are comic books based on a

German cartoon version of *Alice*; one is a Disney adaptation of *Alice im Wunderland* for very young readers; and, the other is this lovely little *Snark*."

"No first edition anywhere in the solar system?"

"Not even one. Zip. Zilch. Nada."

"Too bad!"

"A genuine tragedy. Anyway, the inscription in this one is quite amusing. She jokes with Pasterny about his storing his valuable Carroll collection in his kitchen cabinets. Can you read German?"

"Of course. My parents were German. We spoke it at home." He handed the book to her as carefully as if he were handling nitroglycerine. The last thing he wanted to do was to drop it and bump a corner. That could easily take ₦10,000 off of its value.

"What a wonderful little book!" she said as she studied the cover. Then she opened it and silently read the inscription. She laughed. "You're right; it's very funny! She obviously had a good sense of humour. Do you suppose that he really kept his Carroll collection in his kitchen cabinets?"

"It's hard to believe that anyone would do that. Perhaps it was just a joke between them and he really didn't."

"He probably got away with doing just that by never cooking anything; typical bachelor behaviour."

"That's a better explanation than I could come up with. You're probably right. I think he *was* a bachelor."

Dayna spent the next few minutes looking through the book, oooing and awing all the while. "Lovely," she said as she handed it back to him. "What do you know about Frau Wagner?"

"Not much, really. She supposedly started collecting Carroll rather late in life, but still managed to build one of the great German Carroll collections of the twentieth century—pre-Ice Age, of course."

"What happened to it? Under the glacier somewhere?"

"Probably; just about everything in Europe is. The last I heard they think that the European glacier is now over a kilometre thick. It's astonishing how quickly the ice spread when the Earth's polarity reversed in mid-winter! There wasn't even time—or the means—to evacuate most people to southern latitudes. Personally, I think it's more likely that her descendants burned her books trying to keep warm. As you probably know, almost everything that could burn—including books and furniture—that people could get their hands on was burned, as they futilely tried to avoid freezing to death. Even the British Library's vast holdings went up in smoke! What a loss! But I can't blame the people who burned them; they were desperate. I might have done the same thing—but the Carroll books would have been the last ones that I would have tossed onto the grate."

"Personally, I would rather quickly freeze than slowly starve," she said.

"I agree; much less painful."

"Perhaps they put the really rare things—like their Shakespeare's first folios and the Gutenberg Bible—in a vault."

"Maybe. I would like to think that they saved the *Alice* manuscript as well—but I doubt it."

"Surely they wouldn't have burned it! It was such a small thing. It would have hardly even been worth burning—just a few minutes of heat."

He shrugged. "I hope you're right. Anyway, we'll never know. Perhaps in some distant millennium—once the ice retreats again—those humans living in the planetary colonies can return to search for things like that."

"But the thaw might take tens of thousands of years! I'm sure you know that once an ice age takes hold it takes a very long time for the glaciers to melt again. Human life might not even exist that long—even on Mars or the moons of Jupiter—anywhere for that matter!"

"You're right, of course, unless they can finally figure out how to travel into other dimensions. It's no sure thing." He decided to change the subject and held up another book. "This little gem is Kimie Kusumoto's translation of *Alice's Adventures in Wonderland.* Sadly, I can't read Japanese, so I can't enjoy the translation, but it's gloriously illustrated by the English artist Brian Partridge. There are three known surviving copies of this edition, but this is the only one that's inscribed by Kusumoto. Some guy named Birenbaum in the Io colony has one inscribed by Partridge to the famous English Carroll collector Edward Wakeling. I've tried to buy it from him, but I can't afford it. He's asking ₦400,000."

She laughed. "You're kidding! How could a book be worth that much?"

"That's not an unusual price for an older Carroll edition that has some association value."

"Really?"

"Really." He opened the book to the back to show her Kusumoto's inscription. "I'm told that it's to her friend and fellow collector, Yoshiyuki Momma. He built a fabulous collection of Japanese Carrollian editions back in the mid- to late-1900s." He handed the book to her. "This inscription is evidently very formal—no jokes; the Japanese way."

"Do you know what happened to Momma's collection?"

"No. I doubt that anyone knows. My guess is that it probably burned in the fires that ravaged Honshū when Mount Fuji erupted in 2018, the result of a series of major earthquakes triggered by nuclear warfare in Korea and China. I doubt that anything as delicate and combustible as books would have survived the resultant firestorms."

"Well, this one obviously did!"

"The only reason it did was because it had been sold to a New Zealand collector some years earlier."

"Is that who you bought it from?"

"I wish! It would have been a lot cheaper if I had. I bought it from a rare book dealer in Argentina. I'm not sure how he managed to get hold of it."

Dayna slowly turned though the book, studying each of the intricate drawings. "It's so beautiful!" she gushed. "One can't look at these drawings and not be saddened, knowing that the England he depicted so beautifully is lost forever!"

Captain Boulanger nodded. "Not as pretty as France, of course, but still lovely in places."

When she had finished looking through the book she handed it back. "Who owns the third surviving copy?"

"A billionaire collector that lives in one of the colonies on Ganymede. He'll never part with it. Money means nothing to him; he has more than he knows what to do with! A person would have to kill him to get it."

"What's his name? I might know him. I've made a few trips there and met a number of the colonials," she lied.

"Lindebaum; I forget his first name. Something that begins with a 'J'; Jon or Jacob I think. Sorry, I can't recall it at the moment."

"I met a Jon there once," she lied. "I'll have to look him up the next time I'm there. See if he will show me his Carroll collection."

"If you wear that dress he just might." He held up the next book, which was badly worn and soiled. The once light-green cloth had faded to grey. "This is the 1916 reprinting of *The Story of Sylvie and Bruno*. It's obviously in terrible condition, but it's unique."

"To put it bluntly, François, it looks like crap. I hope you didn't pay a lot for that one. I've never even heard of *Sylvie and Bruno*."

"It was never a popular book; everyone agrees that it was Carroll's great failure. I imagine that most people could care less that every other copy of the *Sylvie and Bruno* books except this one was evidently destroyed."

"Fire or ice?"

"Neither. People just threw them away."

She laughed.

"Still, some of the nonsense poems are good, and I like a few of Furniss' illustrations." He handed the book to her.

"So where did this copy come from? A rubbish bin?"

"Almost. Some guy name Howick found it in a livestock shed in Australia on some remote sheep station in the Outback. I used to know the name, but it slips my memory at the moment; Woola-woola or Bunga-bunga or something like that; one of those funny Aussie names. Actually, most of the surviving Carroll books come out of Australia. It's one of the few places on Earth that wasn't devastated by one of the big natural catastrophes or the nuclear wars. Fortunately, it isn't radioactive."

"That's comforting!" She read a few of the poems aloud and they both laughed at them. "Yes, I agree; they *are* funny!"

"My favourite is the one about the three badgers. It's actually a subtle murder mystery."

"Really?"

"I'll explain it to you sometime if you want to hear about it, but not tonight." He held up the next book. "This is perhaps the strangest Carroll book that I own, called *In the Boojum Forest*. It contains a number of short stories by a little-known American eccentric named Sewell. The darkest and most terrifying story is entitled 'Atchafalaya Boojum'. Most Carrollians maintain that he must have been high on hallucinogenic drugs when he wrote it, but I doubt it. It's more likely that he was just mildly paranoid-schizophrenic. Anyway, it's classic Snarkian horror."

"What's it about?"

"It's about a legendary monster that the local citizens in a coastal Louisiana town. They nicknamed it 'Boojum'—a sort of tyrannosaurus lookalike—that lived deep in the nearby swamp. The Boojum would come out every few years to feed on unsuspecting fishermen. If you encountered him you almost invariably vanished, so to speak."

"Into its stomach?"

"Exactly. Makes you want to stay out of swamps."

"That's definitely one of the rules *I* live by. Rule No. 42: Stay out of swamps."

He grinned. "I've only read the story once. It gave me nightmares—or hallucinations; I'm not sure which."

"Like what, exactly?"

"This will be hard to believe, but it's the truth. I swear it. I was reading it aloud one night, for the entertainment of doing it, with all of the lights out except the reading light over my bunk. Just as I was almost to the end of the story I heard a terrifying, deep growl come from the darkened corner of my room. It scared me more than anything I have ever experienced in my life."

Dayna giggled. "Monsters under your bed, Captain?"

"No; it was a monster in the corner."

"Why didn't you just switch on the light and see what it was?"

"I did."

"What did you see?"

"Sewell's Boojum. A smallish *T. rex* lookalike. About two metres high. Big teeth. Small forelegs. Black and scaly. Long tail."

"Yeah, right!"

"I'm sure it was a hallucination, but it looked very real. I still sleep with the lights on now and with a LP17 sidearm under my pillow. Fortunately, it hasn't returned—yet."

"I'm sure it was just a trick your mind played on you; power of suggestion and all that."

"That's what I tell myself, but I haven't managed to really convince myself yet."

She decided that a touch of dementia might be setting in and wondered if he was truly capable of being captain of the ship. "So, what else did Sewell write?"

"Lots of equally strange stuff. There's a number of collections of some of his short stories that were published by a press called Evertype, now in holobook format of course. The originals, except this one, have all disappeared. Most of his stories aren't quite as a dark and depressing as this one, though there are a few that might qualify. He seemed to have been strangely obsessed with *The Hunting of the Snark*."

"So what happened to him?"

"The widely-held assumption is that he wouldn't have survived the ash cloud from the eruption of the Yellowstone volcano in 2020; few elderly Americans did, especially those downwind, where he lived. He would have been about 80, I guess."

She flipped through the book and handed it back to him after only a quick glance. "Hardly any pictures in this one," she said. "As Alice observed, what's the use of a book without pictures and conversation?"

"It has lots of conversation," he said in its defence, "but you're right; not so many pictures. Okay, last, but not least, there is this very strange cookbook." He held it up so she could see the cover. "*Alice Eats Wonderland.* It's full of disgusting— yet fascinating—recipes for cooking many of the creatures in the *Alice* books."

"And *you* think that the 'Atchafalaya Boojum' is dark?"

"They're both dark, but there are a few significant differences. This cookbook is funny; there's nothing funny about Sewell's swampy tale, and when you read this one you don't have hallucinations of the scary kind." He handed her the cookbook.

"Who were Alison Tannenbaum and August A. Imholtz, Jr.?"

"Two very interesting Americans. Tannenbaum was a brain surgeon and a road-kill taxidermist. Her husband, Alan, built a famous Carroll collection. It's now somewhere under the North American Ice Sheet. Imholtz was a linguist and humorist—an expert in Latin and ancient Greek. Also fluent in German. Taught himself Russian, just for the fun of it. He is said to have owned the largest collection of Russian Carroll editions in America. He co-authored some of Sewell's stranger stories. Have you ever read 'Gone Sideways'?"

"No, but I've seen the film version."

"Sewell and Imholtz collaborated on that story."

"It looks like the previous owner of this book tried some of the recipes—unless it was you that did this damage!"

"It definitely wasn't me. It has to be contemporary."

"Well, whoever it was left some stains on a few pages—like this one right here." She held it up to show him. "This was probably red wine. The real stuff; not the chemical crap *we* know. And that spot right there looks like grease."

"Yes, it is. I had the DNA on it analysed some years ago. They said it was rabbit."

"White Rabbit, by any chance?"

He laughed at her little joke. "Perhaps."

"François, this book's in pretty bad shape, you know."

"I know, but I don't mind most of its problems. What I don't like is the faint odour of garlic. It just never seems to go away. Garlic on food is good. Garlic—like mildew—on books is bad."

"Perhaps it came from Pasterny's collection."

"He didn't cook, remember?"

"Oh! That's right! I forgot. How much did you pay for it—if you don't mind my asking—you don't have to tell me, of course. I'm just curious."

"The dealer that had it was asking ₦285,000. I figured that was a fair price, but I also figured he was desperate to sell it. He had cancer and lots of medical bills. I got him down to ₦137,000, because of the food stains and garlic. It was a real bargain!"

Dayna's jaw had dropped. "That much?"

"Yeah. I could hardly believe that I managed to get it so cheap!"

"That's not what I meant. I was thinking that you probably paid about ₦150 for it. By the way, I was guessing high, since you've obviously lost your perspective on the true value of used books."

He laughed loudly. "You are *so* funny, Dayna! Beautiful and funny. Those days of cheap books are long gone!"

"So, what do you think your collection might be worth then?"

"It's insured for ₦1.5 million, but the value keeps increasing. I need to see about insuring it for a bit more once we get back to Mars. My guess is that it might be worth as much as ₦1.8 million now."

"Why so much? You could buy your own asteroid for that much. I don't get it."

"There are lots of people—very rich people, anyway—who would like to collect Carroll, but there just aren't that many older copies of any of his books that survived. A few get discovered every month or so in the southern climes, but not many. Even an old Disney edition that might have originally cost a few Old Dollars can now fetch a few thousand New Dollars."

"Well then, it's easy to see why you keep them in a safe."

"I just hope that nothing ever happens to them. They're simply irreplaceable, no matter how much money a person might have."

"Which one do you value the most?"

"Oh, I couldn't say. It would be like asking a mother which of her five children she values the most. But, as you might guess, if someone made me a decent offer for the Sewell, I would probably take it. You interested?"

"No!"

"That's right! Not many pictures; I forgot. I'd be willing to discount it a bit because of that."

"No. Definitely no. Let's drink a toast to your amazing collection, Captain Boulanger," she said, retrieving the bottle and plastic glasses from the floor. She pushed the bottle across the table to him.

"You're supposed to call me François!"

"This will be a formal toast!"

"Oh. Well then, all right. It'll take me a minute to find the corkscrew. I don't have many opportunities to use it these days." He took the bottle with him. "I'll just step over there to open it; I wouldn't want to spill any more wine on that cookbook!"

While he was struggling with the cork, Dayna retrieved a syringe from her purse and squirted a few drops into one of the glasses. She slid the glass over to where he had been sitting and then quickly put the syringe back in her purse.

In a minute or two he had finally managed to open the bottle. "A dry cork," he explained, a bit embarrassed that he hadn't been able to just yank it out without half trying. "Getting old, I'm afraid; losing some of my arm strength, I guess."

"No worry, mate. You look fit to me." She held up her empty glass and smiled as he filled it. He quickly filled his own.

"To Captain François Boulanger of the *UNIS Forks and Hope*, and to the immortal Lewis Carroll for whom it was named, and to his muse, little Alice Liddell," she said, lifting her glass.

"To Fusion Reaction Specialist—first class in that dress, I might add—Dayna Keiner, and the Reverend Mr Charles Dodgson and his snarks!" he responded. "Or is it Mr Reverend? I can never remember!"

They clunked their plastic glasses together and then emptied them in one extended drink, while staring deeply into each other's eyes. He loved what he thought he saw. She couldn't have cared less.

"That's a lovely wine!" he said. "What's the batch number?"

She read the label aloud. "GHT89560. I was told that the GHT80000 series is one of the best. It doesn't have that strong copper aftertaste taste you sometimes get."

"Very nice indeed! No coppery taste. Brilliant!"

He started to return the books to the safe, but she placed her hand on his arm. "Could I have a second look at the Japanese book before you lock them back up? Please. Pretty please."

"Of course," he said. "Take as long as you like. I'll just have a bit more 89560 while you're at it." He took the book from the stack and handed it back to her.

After she had looked at it for about five minutes Captain Boulanger suddenly said, "I'm not really feeling wellll—dizzy—thi—" He tried to stand up, but abruptly collapsed to the floor.

She waited a few minutes and then went over and knelt down to check for a pulse in his neck. There was none. "That was your boojum, Captain François," she said aloud, as if he could hear her. A moment later she stood back up and corrected herself. "No, actually, François, *I'm* your boojum."

She quickly stuffed the books into her purse. She went across the small cabin and closed the door to the safe, then punched a few random keys to reset the lock. Since she was still wearing the cotton gloves, she didn't have to worry about fingerprints. She collected the half-empty wine bottle and glasses and left. She was back in her cabin ten minutes later. She put the books in her own safe before finishing off the wine, drinking straight from the bottle to be sure that she didn't make a mistake and drink from the now lethal glass. She then sent the bottle, glasses, and gloves down the disposal tube. They would be automatically shredded to a size of 0.3 microns and injected into the fusion exhaust.

When the Captain hadn't reported to the flight deck the next morning, a squad was sent to his cabin. When there was no response to persistent loud knocking, they sent for a mechanic to open the door. They found the Captain unresponsive on the floor next to the table. The flight surgeon arrived a short time later and pronounced him dead. His body was bagged and removed to a secure refrigerated vault. The cabin was sealed. There would be a forensic investigation and an inquest once they had arrived on still-distant Mars.

Three weeks later, still en route to Mars, Specialist Keiner turned out all of the cabin lights except the small pin-point reading light directly over her pillow and crawled into her bunk with the copy of Sewell's *In the Boojum Forest*. She decided to read it aloud and was almost at the end of the story when she heard it—a very deep and menacing growl—from the darkest corner of her cabin. It was only then that she recalled what the Captain had told her, which was too late. There was no laser weapon under her pillow, and the Boojum looked hungry.

Chapter 11

Snark Eggs and Spam

"*D*r Wahnsinn will see you now, Specialist Keiner." Dayna Keiner acknowledged the receptionist with a nod as she stood up and followed her through a small anteroom into the doctor's office. Dr Wahnsinn, who had been reviewing her medical file on his computer screen, looked up as she came in. He stood and extended his hand. "Guten Morgen, Frau Keiner," he said brightly with a perfect German accent, extending his hand.

She shook his hand as she said, "That's *Specialist* Keiner to you," she said. "*Frau* is inappropriate for a senior officer. And let's stick to English, okay?"

"But of course. My apologies. I had understood that you were fluent in German."

"I am, but I prefer English after so many years away from home."

"I see. My English is not so good, but I will do my best. Please, Specialist Keiner, sit down." He motioned to the only chair in the room, which was directly in front of his large desk, which was completely bare except for his laptop and a 250-millimetre-long vicious-looking fish fossil.

"What is that?" she asked pointing at the fossil.

"That's an Ionian Sumpfish. Perhaps 500,000 years old. Quite rare. Most specimens have only broken teeth. They are needle-like and break easily."

"I've never seen a fish with so many teeth!"

"Yes. Many teeth."

"Why do they call it a sumpfish?"

"I have no idea. I see from your file that you have been suffering from disturbing hallucinations, yes?"

She nodded. "They are persistent and hyper-real. I'm finding it very difficult to sleep, and the loss of sleep is making it difficult for me to perform my job at a satisfactory level. I don't want to get grounded."

"I see. When did these hallucinations begin?"

"About two months ago, three weeks out from our docking on Mars."

"The *UNIS Forks and Hope*, it says here on your chart. A strange name, I think. Do you know what this "forks and hope" means?"

"It's a line from a famous Victorian poem."

"Who was this poet?"

"Look, I'm not here to discuss poetry."

"Sorry, I was just trying to break the ice into tiny little bits. You seem very stressed. Please, tell me exactly what you saw in the first hallucination. I see from your file an admission report at the ER when you arrived here on Mars-14. It mentions something about a 'boojum'. What is this 'boojum'?"

"I called it a boojum, because it looked rather like a monster described in a book I was reading at the time I saw it."

"Please describe for me its appearance—as best you can remember it."

"It looked something like a *Deinonychus*."

"That's a bit too specific. Which planet or moon does it inhabit?"

"Its habitat was Earth in the mid-Cretaceous. It looks something like a *Velociraptor*."

"Still too specific, I'm afraid. Sorry; I am not an expert palaeontologist. Mostly I know about ancient fishes."

"Are you familiar with the old classic film Jurassic Park?"

"Yes; I've seen it a couple times—maybe three time. I was very disappointed that it did not have any of the prehistoric fishes. Still, it was pretty good. I liked the part where the *Tyrannosaurus* eats the man sitting on the toilet. Very funny!"

"*Velociraptor* is what they called the medium-sized dinosaurs in the movie. But what was depicted was not very accurate. Those in the film looked more like *Deinonychus*. The one that I saw in my cabin—and sometimes still see—is about two-meters tall and black, with a long, animated tail and very large hind legs with huge curved claws. It has small forelegs and a mouth full of 150-millimetre-long dagger-like teeth. It's quite terrifying, actually. Believe me!"

"I believe you. And you said that it appeared all of a sudden in your cabin?"

"Yes. It was if it had materialized out of thin air. I heard a deep rumbling growl coming from a dark corner and turned on the lights. It looked very real—and hungry. I lost control of my bladder, unfortunately. It was that frightening."

"Oh, dear! Then you must have been very frightened indeed by such an occurrence."

"I was certain that it intended to eat me!"

"Eat you?"

"Yes, eat me. What would you have thought in my situation?"

"I honestly don't know. You heard it growl and it looked very real—alive, yes?"

"Yes. It looked very much alive. Not a hologram. Alive."

"Could you also smell it?"

"No. That's why I thought that it might just be a hallucination." She didn't mention that Captain Boulanger had also seen it and described it to her. Since there was no such thing as doctor-patient confidentiality on Mars, she naturally didn't want anyone to make a connection between her and the late Captain.

"So, you were reading the *Jurassic Park* at the time?"

"No, I was reading a short story by an obscure pre-Ice Age author."

"What was this author's name?"

"You won't recognize it."

"I might."

"Okay. It was Sewell."

"But I do know that name! But I think she was a writer of horse stories for children. Black something or other. I forget it."

"Wrong Sewell. This one was Byron Sewell; no relation to Anna. And this was no children's story, I can assure you."

"What was the title? Perhaps I've heard of it."

"No way."

"I'm well read. I might have."

"All right. It was 'Atchafalaya Boojum'."

"Hmm. No, this title I do not know. What language was it written in?"

"Mostly English—and a little Cajun French. Atchafalaya was the name of a swamp in what was once known as Louisiana. It's now under the North American Ice Sheet where, in my opinion, it belongs. A 'boojum' is a mythical creature invented by the English Victorian author Lewis Carroll. It's a special kind of snark, another word that Carroll invented."

"I thought that snark was just the rude and critical comments spoken by women who hate each other."

"That too, but that's a more modern usage. The word snark is used by Carroll as a sort of generic term for some mythical animals that have tasty meat and are good for striking a light. It also includes one very bad sub-species—called a boojum snark—if you are unfortunate enough to encounter one of those then you suddenly vanish."

"Vanish?"

"Yes. You pass into the void. Nothingness. You vanish. POOF!" She snapped her fingers for emphasis, making him flinch.

"Ahh! Perhaps this is the source of your *angst*—the primeval fear of eventually ceasing to exist—after you die—there is nothing. It's a common fear."

"I don't think so. I travel all of the time through inter-planetary space, which is about as close to being a void as you can get—if you ignore the dark matter that you can't see or feel. What I'm fearful about is being eaten by a *deinonychus*. I realize that this is an irrational fear, but the creature I see looks and sounds very real. In fact I honestly can't distinguish it from reality. The next time I encounter it I might just fire my sidearm at it and if I miss I might puncture the shell of the ship."

"That would be bad!"

"Uh—yeah! *Very* bad!"

"Perhaps you should keep your sidearm locked up in a safe."

"What? And encounter a *Deinonychus* without any way of defending myself?"

"But you seem to realize that it's a hallucination! If it wasn't a hallucination, then why didn't it go ahead and eat you up?"

"Because Security knocked on my cabin door and inter-rupted it. Its head wheeled around and looked at the door. Then it suddenly vanished."

"Poof?"

"Yeah, POOF! It was there one moment and gone the next. Blink of an eye."

"Did you go to the door?"

"Of course."

"And what was there?"

"A marine with his weapon pointed at my chest. I noticed that he had also lost control of his bladder."

"Really?"

"Yes, really! He told me that he was walking by on patrol and heard a terrifying growl. That's why he stopped and knocked. To see if I was all right."

"Are you saying that *he* heard *your* hallucination?"

"Apparently."

"That's pure nonsense! I can believe some impossible things before breakfast, but not that! The security guard must have also been part of your hallucination."

"Look, if you don't believe what I tell you then there's no point in my telling you anything."

"Please, do not misunderstand me. I believe that your brain saw what you say you saw. I just don't believe that it was real."

"He left a puddle on the floor of my cabin entry. Was that also a hallucination?"

"The boojum left a puddle?"

"No! The marine did!"

"Oh! That's different. Okay. I'm going to give you a prescription for a powerful antipsychotic drug. We'll see if that helps, maybe."

"What are its side effects?"

"Pretty scary, really; but not as scary as what you are experiencing with this boojum thing! We can always get you a new liver transplanted if the drug destroys the one you've got. We don't want you out there somewhere in space pumping holes in the shells of your spaceship, now, do we?"

"No. We certainly don't want that. That's why I'm here."

"If I were you I wouldn't go reading 'Atchafalaya Boojum' no more. Especially at night with the lights out."

"Not a problem! I hope to sell it."

"Don't wait to try to sell it. Just go home and throw it away! Do it tonight! Why wait?"

"I can't do that. It's too valuable."

"How valuable could it be?"

"It depends on the buyer. I can probably get ₦200,000; maybe even ₦300,000."

"You're kidding!"

"No."

"Who in their right minds would pay so much for a stupid book?"

"Some guy on Ganymede might be interested—if you're not."

"Me? Interested? Definitely not! I don't make that much money in even two years! And I'm a doctor! They pay me well."

"That would be more like five years' salary for me. That's why I can't just simply throw it away. I have an idea. Why don't you conduct a little experiment with it?"

"Like what?"

"You could read it and see what happens for yourself—see if you see any prehistoric monsters—or perhaps a big fish with lots of needles for teeth."

He thought for a moment. "That would indeed be an interesting thing to do, but I can't afford it."

"I'll make it easy for you. I'll bring the book by and you can read it for yourself—no charge."

"You could leave it with me."

"No. It's too valuable. I would insist that I stay in the room with it while you read it. We can share impressions if the boojum or a big sumpfish swims by and we both see it."

He thought again for a few moments. "You don't trust me?"

"Not with my ₦300,000 book, no."

"All right. When can you bring it by?"

"Tomorrow night. Let's say 19:00."

"Good. I will let you in. Just knock the door."

She got up to leave. He handed her the prescription. "Don't take this until we have conducted our little experiment. You will see that nothing happens. Then perhaps you will believe that it is just your imagination running wild around inside your brain, with the scary thoughts giving you angst."

"We'll see," she said as she left.

The next night she knocked on Dr Wahnsinn's office door at precisely 19:00. A few moments later the door opened. "Come in Specialist Keiner; come in." He gestured towards his office. "I believe you know the way. I see that you're armed. Are you making plans to shoot the monster?"

"I might be," she said as she sat down in the chair in front of his desk. "But I actually came armed in case you decided to try to steal my ₦300,000 book."

He laughed. She didn't.

"You are serious?" he asked.

"Quite serious." There was no hint of a smile on her face.

"I assure you, Specialist Keiner, that I have no intentions of stealing your book!" He sat down in his own chair behind the desk. "So, did you bring the book?"

"Of course." She pulled it out of her purse and placed it on top of the desk in front of him. "Be careful with it. Don't bend any pages. Treat it like your life depended on it. It just might."

"What if I sneeze on top of it or make the little smudges or something?"

"I'll shoot you in the leg if you do."

"You'll shoot me? Are you serious?"

"Yes. Just be careful."

"Take it easy! Whoa! Such aggression! Perhaps your testosterone levels are out of whack!"

"Could be, so be careful or—" she brought up her finger as if it were a pistol and pointed it at his head. *"Bang!"*

He involuntarily jumped.

"Just read the dang book!" she demanded. "Read it aloud!"

"Okay. Okay. Don't get the so excited. I won't hurt the book." He opened it and started to read, but she interrupted him. "You need to turn out all of the lights except that small lamp over your desk."

"Why?"

"It's an experiment. We need to replicate the conditions as best we can."

"I doubt that this will be necessary, but I will humour you. I don't want you to shoot me or something!" He flipped a few switches embedded in the desktop and all of the lights went out with the exception of the lamp. "There," he said. "All right now?"

"Just one more thing," she said. She stood up and shoved her chair away from the desk, back close to the door.

"Why did you do that?" he asked.

"When the boojum shows up I want to be as far away as possible and very near the door—just in case."

The doctor smiled, humouring her. "Now, Dayna—"

"Don't call me Dayna!"

"Sorry. I forgot. Don't shoot! You will soon see that this is all in your imagination. You'll see. There is no such boojum thing running around and poofing out of the air."

It took him about an hour to read the story. When he had finished he turned up the lights and noticed that Dayna had her sidearm at the ready. "Please, Specialist Keiner, holster your weapon! It might go off by accident. There is no boojum in here. I read the book. Nothing happened. Just like I told you. Nothing. Just quiet."

She didn't say anything for a minute; still on alert.

"It is a terrifying story," he continued, "but that's all—just a scary story. Not real." He came around the desk and handed her the book, which she returned to her purse. "Please notice. No bends to the pages. No sneezing all over it. Just as when you gave it to me. Yes?"

She nodded. "Well, I must admit that I'm relieved," she said. "I was certain that it would reappear. I suppose you're right. It must just have been a hallucination." Even though she said this, she didn't really believe it.

She started to push the chair back, but he stopped her. "Don't bother. I will do that." He extended his hand, which she took and shook. "Please, take your weapon and hurry away so that I won't have a bullet sticking out of my brain or something!"

"Okay. Thank you, Doctor."

"You're welcome. Be sure to fill the prescription as soon as you can and don't stop taking the medicine without checking with me first. Don't overdose on it. Watch out for indications of hepatic failure."

She nodded and left. She had no intention of taking the medicine. She wasn't about to risk destroying her liver.

The next morning, as she was brewing what passed on Mars for coffee, she tuned in *Odyssey*, one of the local Martian TV news channels.

"What are believed to be Dr Alan Wahnsinn's remains were discovered by his receptionist, Ms Alison Mastif, at his offices when she arrived at work this morning. The authorities are not revealing many details yet, but one anonymous witness has informed *Odyssey Daily News* that all that was found of Dr Wahnsinn was his head and left foot. His office was said to be awash in blood. Initial reaction is that he may have been attacked by the large Europan Iceworm that hasn't been seen since its strange disappearance from the Interplanetary Zoological Gardens about a week ago. This is an on-going story. Stay tuned to *Odyssey* for regular updates."

"Hallucination, eh?" she said to the screen. "So much for rationality!"

A few minutes later her doorbell rang and she went to see who it was. She checked through the peephole before opening it to be sure there wasn't a boojum standing in the hallway pretending to deliver a pizza. She saw that it was Martian Security. She opened the apartment door. "Yes, officer?"

"Specialist Dayna Keiner?" he asked as he showed her his identification. "I'm Detective Augustus Holtzenheimer."

"Yes, that's me. What do you want?"

"May I come in? I'd like to ask you a few questions."

"Of course." She opened the door wide and he stepped inside. She closed the door and led him into the living room. "Please, take a seat," she said as she sat down on the divan.

"Have you heard the tragic news this morning about Dr Wahnsinn?"

"Yes, just a few minutes ago, actually. It's most disturbing. Nothing left but his head and a foot! I forget which one."

"Left."

"That's right. I remember now. Good grief!"

"Yes, quite horrific. Blood all over the place. We understand that you were one of his patients. Is that correct?"

"Yes."

"When did you see him last?"

She knew that there was no point in lying and that they would have reviewed the hallway CCTV holofiles this morning. "I was at his office last night for an hour or so starting at 19:00."

"Why were you there? Those were not his normal office hours and you aren't listed in his appointment book for that timeframe."

"I've been ill and he wanted to discuss various treatment options. We agreed that I should return last night for further consultation."

"What was the conclusion?"

"He prescribed an antipsychotic drug that he wanted me to try. I'm sure that this would have been recorded on my charts. You can easily verify this."

"We've already reviewed your chart, but there were only a few entries. He was evidently attacked while in the process of writing them up soon after your departure."

"What did you find?"

"Just that he had prescribed Splyne for you. There were also a few cryptic words."

"Spline?"

"Sorry; that's the street name for dioxysplynochol-hydrochloride. It's gives you a euphoric high, but it's also a good way to destroy your liver if you're not careful."

"He told me about the liver. I don't intend to fill his prescription. I like my liver just the way it is, and I don't want yellow eyes. They wouldn't go with my wardrobe."

Detective Holtzenheimer didn't laugh. "Anyway, those strange words that he wrote on your chart are what I wanted to ask you about."

"What were they?" she was becoming very nervous and was struggling to act nonchalant.

"*Atchafalaya* and *boojum*. Does that mean anything to you?"

She swallowed wrong and choked. It took her a few minutes to clear her throat.

"Are you okay?" he asked, once she had recovered enough to talk again. "Should I get you a glass of water?"

"No water. I'm fine. I just swallowed wrong. I hate when I do that. What was it you asked me? I've forgotten."

"*Atchafalaya* and *boojum*. Do they mean anything to you?"

"No, sorry. What language is that?"

"*Atchafalaya* is a Choctaw word."

"Choctaw?"

"A language once spoken by a tribe of Native Americans. According to the *Encyclopaedia Galactica* it means 'long river'. But 'boojum' isn't Choctaw. It's a word coined by Lewis Carroll, the author of a nonsense epic poem entitled *The Hunting of the Snark*. We did some research and discovered that 'Atchafalaya Boojum' was also the name of an obscure short story written about a hundred years ago, set in what used to be called Louisiana before it was covered by the North American Ice Sheet. Any of this mean anything to you?"

"No. Why should it?"

"I don't know. It was just written on your medical chart, so we were hoping that it might mean something to you and that it might provide a clue as to what might have happened to Dr Wahnsinn."

"Perhaps he was eaten by a boojum," she said, smiling.

He didn't find this funny either. "Not too likely. Not on Mars, anyway."

"It was just a thought. Anything else?"

"No, that was it. Thank you for your time."

"I'm sorry that I couldn't have been more help, Detective Weisenheimer."

"It's Holtzenheimer, actually."

"Oh! Sorry. A Freudian slip or something, I guess. Sorry."

"It's okay. I've heard that all of my life. If you think of anything please give me a call." He handed her a business card with his name and phone number.

"I certainly will."

"Well, good day, then" he said as he stood up to leave. "I can see myself out."

Dayna locked the front door behind him and went back to check for any updates on *Odyssey*. "This just in," said a female talking head with blue hair and too much eye makeup.

"The police haven't found any tell-tale slime traces of Europan Iceworm. DNA analysis results of the blood found at the scene will be available later today. Stay tuned for updates." Fifteen minutes later *Odyssey Daily News* interrupted their normal programming of reruns with an urgent update: "*Odyssey Daily News* has just learned that the escaped Europan Iceworm has been recaptured. It was discovered by an employee who went into the walk-in freezer at the MacJovian restaurant on Birenbaum Square to get a box of frozen cloned chicken nuggets. An inventory check indicated that the iceworm had eaten close to 30 kilograms of expensive bison-burger patties. The iceworm has been safely transported back to its enclosure at the Interplanetary Zoological Gardens. It isn't clear how it managed to get into the freezer, but police are questioning another MacJovian employee, who is known as a trafficker of worms—"

"Creep!" Dayna said to the screen and then changed channels to see if there was any news there. She just caught the tail end of a broadcast, "—strange traces of reptile DNA. Stay tuned to *Voyager News* for updates on this developing story. Now back to our regularly sched—" She switched the channel back to *Odyssey*. The blue-haired talking head was back. "DNA analysis indicates a genetic relationship with iguanas, an extinct species of aquatic lizard once found on Earth on the Galapagos Islands."

"Idiot!" Dayna shouted at the screen and then screamed "It's a Boo—" but caught herself just in time, when she remembered that everything said in her apartment was probably recorded.

Over the next few weeks the newsworthiness of the grisly death of Dr Wahnsinn had declined until it was finally dropped. A week later Dayna was informed that she had been assigned as the Fusion Reaction Specialist on a ship making an emergency trip to Ganymede three days hence. The fleet commander was a bit worried about her recent psychotic incidents, but she was the only Fusion Reactor Specialist available and he had no real choice. It might take a month to bring in a replacement Specialist.

Before departing, Dayna went online and searched the Colonist Registry for "LINDEBAUM, Jon" on Ganymede and found his address listed as Cluster 18, Pod 65. There was also a Spacebook site, but she seriously doubted that he would respond positively to some complete stranger wanting to be his friend, so she didn't even bother trying to contact him. Everyone on Ganymede probably wanted to be the friend of a billionaire. She went into her bedroom and put on a wig and dark glasses, retrieved the books and called up the Ganymede Green Pages and looked for antiquarian book dealers. There was only one: *Books, by Jove!*. "What else?" she said aloud. "Just about everything in this place is Jovian-something!" She sent the bookshop a holomail and waited for a response.

Five minutes later her screen lit up with a real-time holo-image of the owner of *Books, by Jove!*. "Hello," a grey-bearded middle-aged man said. He had a kind face and a bright smile. "My name is Mícheál Mac Síoraí. Did you just call *Books, by Jove!*?"

"Yes. I will be travelling to Ganymede soon and wanted to know if you might want to act as my agent for the sale of some books."

"Perhaps. What sort of books do you wish to sell?"

"I have a collection of five very old and rare Lewis Carroll books."

"Are you serious?"

"Yes. They were my grandfather's."

"Can you describe them for me?"

She spent the next few minutes briefly describing them. "Are you interested?"

"How much do you want for them?"

"One million New Dollars."

He laughed. "You can't be serious!"

"Oh, but I am, and I am confident of their value, so don't even think about trying to scam me!"

"There's only one book collector on Ganymede with that sort of money who might be interested," he said.

"Jon Lindebaum."

He looked genuinely startled. "How did you get his name?"

"None of your business. Are you interested or not?"

"I might be."

"I will pay you a commission of twenty percent, so it will be to your advantage to get as high a price as you can."

"How do I know that you really have the books?"

"I'll show them to you."

Dayna then held each book up to the screen in turn and waited a few minutes. "Okay. Did you see them?"

"Yes. It's quite a collection."

"Worth a million?"

"Perhaps. It depends on condition."

"I know. I've taken that into account. Some are a bit rough. If they were in fine condition I would want two million. I assume that Lindebaum is one of your clients."

"Of course."

"I know that he collects rare Carrolliana."

"How could you possibly know that?"

"Look, it's none of your business, okay? I just know. Quit prying or I will bypass you and deal with him directly."

"He doesn't talk to just anyone. You need me more than I need you and—"

She switched off the connection and waited. Fifteen minutes later the screen lit up again with Mac Síoraí's face. "I seem to have gotten off on the wrong foot. Sorry. I'll be happy to act as your agent. I had a brief chat with Mr Lindebaum, who is very interested, even though we both feel your asking price is too high."

"The price is firm. If that's going to be a problem then I'll contact the next collector on my list."

"Please, don't misunderstand. I'm not saying that he wouldn't be willing to pay your asking price if the books are in good condition. It sounds as if the cookbook is a bit of a mess. He simply needs to see the books before he commits. Condition is very important. There may need to be some minor price adjustment. That's all. For example, he might only be interested in buying some of the books."

"It's a package deal. All or nothing."

"But surely—"

"All or nothing. I'll drop by your shop when I get there."

"Bring the books."

"No. I want to meet Lindebaum first; see if I think I can trust him—and you. Arrange for him to drop by your shop in three days. Leave me a message with the time." She hung up again without saying good-bye.

Upon arrival on Ganymede she checked into the Quantum Nights Hotel in Cluster 42. Once she was settled in she put the Carroll books and her sidearm in the room safe and went back down to the lobby where she caught the shuttle train to Cluster 18, about five kilometres away, where it was positioned atop the rim of an ancient, shallow crater, affording spectacular views across the bluish-green ice and ammonia fields. She took a mini-taxi to Pod 65 and quickly found *Books, by Jove!*.

Dayna went inside and was immediately met by the grey-bearded man she recognized as Mícheál Mac Síoraí. "May I help you?" he asked in a friendly tone.

"Perhaps," she said. "I just wanted to look around first and see what sort of titles you have in stock."

"Are you a collector?"

"No. I can't afford to be a collector. However, my fiancé is and I was thinking about possibly buying him a book for his birthday."

"What sort of books does he collect?"

"He likes children's books and hobbits and old comic books."

"He must be wealthy."

"Fabulously," she said, "but I'm not, so I have to find something reasonable."

"Well, I'm sure you realize that all old paper books are rare after the catastrophes on Earth."

"Yes, I know. What do you have for under ₦1,000?"

"Nothing. The cheapest book I have in stock is ₦25,000."

"Oh, dear! Well, just out of curiosity, what would ₦25,000 buy?"

"A copy of *Helen's Babies* that needs rebinding. Unfortunately it doesn't have a cover. The pages are acid-toned and a few of the illustrations have been coloured in by a child. There is also some damp-staining."

"And for that piece of crap you want ₦25,000?"

"That's what I could probably get on eBay.gny."

"Then why not sell it?"

"I need to keep some things in stock."

"Well, what would ₦30,000 get me? Any Lewis Carroll?"

He laughed. "No, the cheapest Lewis Carroll I have is ₦85,000."

"And what might that be?"

"A 310th printing of the Penguin paperback edition of *Through the Looking-Glass*."

"Does it have a frakking cover?" Dayna was getting pretty angry with his overpriced stock.

"Yes, it has a cover, but it is an ex-library book with all of the usual faults. That hurts its value. That's why the price is so low."

"What if—theoretically speaking, you understand—I wanted a fine copy of a beautifully illustrated 2015 edition of *Alice's Adventures in Wonderland* with a pristine paper cover? How much would that set me back?"

"It would depend on the illustrator. But perhaps as much as ₦4,000,000; even more."

"Signed by the illustrator?"

"At least double that, but such things are today practically non-existent this far out in the solar system."

This was great news, but she didn't let on. "That's absurd!"

"Absurd or not, that's the going price on today's market. I saw a Martian catalogue which had one of the Evertype editions with the Stauton illustrations, though."

"Do you have any other Lewis Carroll books in stock?"

"No. I sell them as soon as they come in. There's a high demand for them and a long waiting list."

"*Winnie the Pooh* then?"

"None."

"*Snark Eggs and Spam?*"

"Nothing."

"Any pretty old *Hobbit* editions?"

"Odd you should ask. I do in fact have one for ₦750,000. It's a Cornish translation. Any interest in that?"

"No. That's way beyond my means unless you might be willing to take my grandkids in trade?"

He laughed. "I haven't met a child yet that is worth half that much!"

"You haven't met my grandkids, Jada and Kiki. They're both worth their weight in Lewis Carroll books!"

He smiled. "Not to me. Are you a stand-up comedian?"

"No, I'm a fusion reactor specialist."

He laughed. "Yeah, right! Very funny!"

She turned to go.

"Thanks for dropping by. I didn't get your name."

"That would probably be because I didn't give it to you."

"Probably. Please let me know if you change your mind about *The Hobbit*."

She smiled and left.

CHAPTER III

Snark and Swiss
on Rye

*T*wo days after her reconnaissance of the Ganymede bookshop, *Books, by Jove!*, Dayna received a holomail message from the shop's owner, Mícheál Mac Síoraí. Dayna put on her wig and dark glasses before accepting the message. "Good day, Mr Mac Síoraí," she said in a neutral tone.

"Good day. I'm just calling to let you know that Mr Lindebaum will be in my bookshop tomorrow at 13:30. We will be closed for lunch from twelve to thirteen. Please don't be late. It's not wise to keep a billionaire waiting."

"He's just a billionaire," she said, "not the gorram King of Ganymede!"

"Around here it's pretty much the same thing."

"What if the shuttle is delayed?"

"The shuttle is very dependable. However, it would be prudent to plan on arriving at least 20 minutes early, just in case. In order to demonstrate your good faith in this transaction, you should bring along one of the books that you showed me online earlier. Mr Lindebaum wants to personally examine it."

"Which one?"

"It's your choice, but I would suggest one of the better ones. It will make a better impression."

"Okay, but anything happens to the book or to me while I'm there then I will withdraw the sell offer."

"There will be no problems from us. We can make other arrangements to transfer the books and payment later if he is interested in proceeding. Good-bye."

She clicked off without saying good-bye. The conversation left her with a bad feeling about the arrangement. She didn't like the idea of his insistence that she take the shuttle. She could imagine someone waiting in the shuttle car to rob her of the book. She decided to arrange for a security escort. She called "No Worries", a local security firm founded by a former Australian commando. They advertised that they employed ex-military special ops. Dayna arranged for two fully-armed bodyguards to pick her up at the hotel and escort her to the bookstore.

The next day she put on her wig and dark glasses and met her escorts in the lobby at 12:00. They were easy to spot in their full combat gear, including body armour and helmets. She noted that they were armed with state-of-the-art particle-beam weapons suitable for either close-quarter combat or disabling a tank if necessary.

They arrived at *Books, by Jove!* at 13:01 and walked in. Mac Síoraí and another older man were standing at the back of the shop talking quietly about something. Two burly men in dark suits, who were obviously Lindebaum's bodyguards, were standing nearby. When her escort stepped forward the two men in dark suits moved between them and Lindebaum and placed their hands inside their coats in a threatening manner. Dayna's bodyguards spun their weapons around, pointing at the dark-suits. They wisely eased their hands back out from inside their jackets.

Dayna ignored Mac Síoraí and calmly walked past the dark-suits to Lindebaum with her hand extended. "You must be Mr Lindebaum," she said. "It's a pleasure to meet you."

He was a small man with thinning grey hair, a sharp nose and a weak chin. He shook her hand. "You seem to have been expecting trouble," he observed.

She shrugged. "Even one book is valuable. I don't know you, so I thought it would be prudent to come prepared for whatever might happen. Better safe than sorry, as they say."

"Nothing will happen," he assured her.

"Mr Mac Síoraí indicated that you wanted to see one of my books. I brought this one along." She handed him her purse. "You can take it out yourself. I don't want your two gorillas to get too nervous."

"They're always nervous. It's their job." He opened the purse and took out the Insel *Snark*. He quickly examined it. "This is a fine copy. Can I ask you where you got it?"

"You can ask, but I won't tell you."

"Are the other four books in similar condition?"

"Unfortunately, not all of them. A few have various problems, and *Alice Eats Wonderland* is in admittedly poor shape. Still, as far as I am aware, the darkly comic cookbook is the only known surviving copy."

"Mr Mac Síoraí informed me that you want one million for the lot."

"That's correct."

"I can offer you ₦850,000."

"I explained to Mr Mac Síoraí that the price was non-negotiable. What I am asking is fair market value and reflects the conditions of all five books."

"He told me. It's too high."

"Then we're done." She reached over and jerked back the book and her purse, turned around and headed for the door.

"Wait!" Lindebaum said. "I'll give you ₦900,000, but that's my best offer."

She didn't even look back and led the way out of the bookshop with her bodyguards protectively following her, walking backwards with their weapons aimed at the two gorillas in monkey suits. Back in the hotel she returned the book to the safe. She waited three hours, put on her wig and dark glasses and located a public holomessage booth, from which she contacted Mr Mac Síoraí. "I thought you understood that the price was firm."

"That's what I told Mr Lindebaum, but he's not used to someone telling him that an offer he makes is unacceptable. Frankly, he's as frumious as a Bandersnatch. Bad things usually happen to anyone who refuses one of his offers."

"I figured that he would try some stunt like that. That's why I showed up with my friends. I'm as frumious as he is. Maybe even frumiouser!"

"You really should have accepted his offer. It was close to what you were asking."

"Not close enough. I hold you responsible for not making that perfectly clear to him."

"Oh, he understood. He just didn't like it. My advice to you is to take your books and leave Ganymede at the first opportunity. He will inevitably locate you—this is a relatively small place—and take possession of the books—one way or another—if you get my drift."

"Are you saying that I'm in danger?"

"Probably. What's more, he asked me to inform you that if I heard from you again that his offer is now ₦500,000. Take my good advice; accept it or leave."

"Get back to him and tell him that my new offer is ₦1.1 million. It will be good for twenty-four hours starting from right now. What I am asking is pocket change for him and it's a fair price. After that I will make no further attempts at contacting either of you. The books will leave Ganymede."

"Okay. I'll call in a few hours and let you know if he's interested. He won't be happy to hear that you've raised the price."

"Too bad. Tell the big baby to get over it. Tell him those were my exact words."

"You're either very brave, stupid, or a fool. Maybe all three."

"Here's the deal if he wants the books. Leave a non-refundable interplanetary electronic funds transfer card for ₦1.1 million less a ten-percent commission, for 'Bearer' in your shop no later than 13:00 tomorrow. I'll verify that the card's good and if it is then I'll tell you where the books are. If your shop is closed the deal is off."

"Our deal was a twenty-percent commission."

"That was before you screwed up."

There was a moment of silence while he thought it over. "He won't go for it."

"Then he won't get the books and you won't get your ₦110,000 commission."

"Oh, he'll get the books—on his terms."

"Dream on, sweet little Alice." She hung up.

Dayna checked out of the hotel and returned to the spaceship, which was docked in a high security military zone, so that she wouldn't have to worry about any of Lindebaum's goons tracking her down. Security personnel at the spaceport were under orders to use lethal force if necessary to stop any unauthorized persons trying to enter the area, a precaution necessary to fend off would-be space pirates, who on rare occasion foolishly tried to take a ship. They invariably failed and all that remained of them were small piles of greyish pirate-ash and puddles of radioactive molten metal from what used to be their weapons.

The next day she again arranged for a "No Worries" escort to pick her up, this time just outside the spaceport perimeter. She put the books in an ordinary plastic shopping bag, this one decorated with the iconic image of Johnny Depp's Hatter primly drinking tea from a small porcelain teacup. She put her sidearm in her purse just in case something went terribly wrong and she needed to defend herself. She donned her wig and dark glasses and went down to the spaceport guard house. Her escorts arrived in an armoured vehicle disguised to look like an ordinary taxi. They stopped well back from the perimeter fence so as not to a trigger a security alert in the spaceport. Dayna walked out to the taxi and climbed inside. They left immediately for *Books, by Jove!* at just below the speed limit.

About 30 metres from the bookstore a policeman stepped out into the street and signalled that they should stop. When he looked inside and saw the armed escort he reached for his sidearm. The driver slammed the door into him, knocking him to the pavement and breaking his right arm. He was then quickly out of the taxi and all over him like warm butter on toast. He looked back at Dayna and said, "We should probably abort. I know this guy. He's not a policeman. He works for Lindebaum. If you go inside the bookstore you probably won't come out with your life. That might apply to us as well. There's no way to know how many others are inside and how well armed they might be. But it's your call. We can't guarantee your safety in this situation."

"All right. Abort!"

Her escort jerked the costumed policeman over to the curb, got back in the vehicle and did a fast one-eighty. They sped away at high speed, swerving back and forth like a drunk driver to dodge any incoming beams. As Dayna looked out the rear window she saw two men emerge from the shop firing laser pistols. One beam glanced harmlessly off of the taxi's roof. The others missed completely. The next moment they made a sharp turn and were out of harm's way. She was safely back on the ship twenty minutes later.

The next day Dayna left the spaceship without her normal disguise and caught the shuttle back to *Books, by Jove!* She took the copy of *In the Boojum Forest* with her, along with her laser sidearm, both stashed in her purse. Thirty minutes later she walked back into the shop, where she found Mac Síoraí sitting at a small desk in front of his computer. He glanced up when she came in. "Ah!" he said. "The *Hobbit* lady is back. Come in. I'll just be a moment. I need to place a call."

"Is it all right if I look at the books in your cases?"

"Of course. They're all locked, but I can let you see anything you would like to see. Just give me a few minutes."

"No problem. I'm not in a hurry." She walked over to the first case and scanned the spines behind the laser-proof glass until she saw *An Hobys*, which she imagined must be the Cornish for *The Hobbit*. Even though Mac Síoraí was speaking in a low voice she could make out his conversation. He was evidently placing a call to her.

"This is Mícheál Mac Síoraí. Please contact me at your earliest convenience about the books. Mr Lindebaum is prepared to accept your offer." He then clicked off and came over to where Dayna was peering intently through the glass.

"I thought you were only interested in low-end books," he said. "The ones in that case start at ₦200,000."

"I've decided that I can afford more than I had originally intended. After all, it's a present for my fiancé, not just some distant cousin. However, I don't have enough for your Cornish *Hobbit*. Still, you tweaked my curiosity about it. Could I see it?"

"Of course, but you can only look; not touch."

"That's fine."

Mac Síoraí slipped on a pair of white cotton gloves and then punched in a code to unlock the door in the case. He reached in and carefully pulled out a leather-bound octavo-sized book, which he then laid on a small table just beneath the wall-mounted case. "Here it is," he said. "I have verified that this is the first, and only edition, published in hardcover and paperback in 2014. Of course it has been rebound now." He opened the book to the two-page map at the front of the book. It featured a pointing hand, mountain, dragon, and some runic inscriptions. "The book is in fine condition. It was rebound by Molniya and Istok, circa 2020. Their binding ticket is on the rear pastedown. I'll show you that in a moment—" When he glanced up he saw that Dayna had her laser pistol aimed at his chest. "What the—"

"I came by yesterday as arranged and instead I found a trap waiting for me."

"Who are you?"

She ignored his question. "I had an idea that you couldn't be trusted."

"You don't look like the woman I've been dealing with."

"Oh, it's me all right. You can't go by appearances."

"What do you want? I don't have the money. Lindebaum never had any intention of paying you."

"Go over and erase everything on your security system."

He laughed. "Hardly."

Without hesitation she shot him in the foot, burning a perfectly round hole eight millimetres in diameter completely through his instep and leaving a flash burn on the floor. He fell, screaming in agony. There was no blood, since the beam had seared the flesh.

"I'll put the next beam through your knee if you don't do it immediately."

"Okay. Okay! Don't shoot!" He crawled over to his computer desk.

"Pop the computer case open and pull out the hard drive. Toss it over here. Do it now or you'll soon have another hole through some other painful part of your scrawny anatomy."

It took him a few minutes to pull out the hard drive. He slid it over to her. "Now go over to your security system and pull out the discs. Toss them over here as well." He did as he was told, very worried about the possibility of a hole through his knee. "Now, stand back from the computer," she ordered. He pulled back and she shot the computer, which quickly melted.

"Come back over here next to the *Hobbit* book and stand with your back to wall. Put your hands on your head and interlock your fingers. Do it!"

He hobbled over and complied.

"If you move when I don't tell you to, you're dead."

"I won't move."

She reached over to *An Hobys* and ripped out the frontis and title page.

Mac Síoraí screamed as if she had just pulled off one of his fingers. "Nooooo! Please don't. Please! The book is worth a small fortune!"

"Shut up!"

For the next few minutes she ripped out every colour illustration, dropping each one onto a growing pile at her feet. With a quick gesture she then pumped a brief laser burst into the pile of pages, burning a hole through them all. "That's for setting me up," she said.

"I'll kill you for doing that to that book!" he snarled and then made a lame attempt to lunge at her. She unhesitatingly put a beam through his head. He was dead before he hit the *Hobbit* pile.

"Jerk!" she snarled and then stepped over his body to the desk, where she left the copy of *Atchafalaya Boojum* in full view. She put a post-it on the cover with Lindebaum's name on it to be sure he would find it. She opened the electronic address book on the desk and found Lindebaum's phone number and gave him a call using the *Books, by Jove!* store phone.

A young woman's voice with a Vietnamese accent answered. "May I help you?"

"Can I leave a message for Mr Lindebaum?"

"Of course. Just a moment while I connect you to his voice-mail."

Dayna listened impatiently through the pointless instructions and then, following the beep, said, "This is the Lewis Carroll lady. I've left one of the books you wanted at *Books, by Jove!*. It's on the desk. You might want to send one of your goons over to collect it for you before the police show up and take it."

She picked up the hard drive and discs, put them in her purse along with her sidearm, and returned to the ship. She had lots to do to ready the fusion reactor for tomorrow's scheduled departure for distant Titania.

CHAPTER IV

Snark Vindaloo

*S*tefan picked up a two-kilogram chunk of Boojum meat and held it up. "Hey, Alan! I wonder what this would taste like?"

"Probably like fishy-chicken. Strange meat invariably tastes like fishy-chicken if it's reptilian or amphibian."

"It'd be a shame not to cook a bit and see."

"What if it's poison?"

"Don't be stupid."

"Well, give a try if you're feeling lucky. I'd suggest vindaloo. We've got vinegar, powdered cayenne pepper, and citric acid. We can probably fake a decent vindy sauce. If it's hot enough it might even cover the fishy-flavour."

"I've noticed that Lindebaum has a small bag of basmati rice in the pantry. Let's ask him if we can eat some of it."

"It probably cost him ₦500 to import it all the way out here to Ganymede."

"I wouldn't be surprised. Still, we just saved his life, so maybe he's feeling generous."

"I'll go check," Alan offered.

"All right. I'll collect the bigger chunks of meat and put them in the freezer, just in case we like it and want some more."

"I doubt it, but who knows?" He went off to find Lindebaum and Stefan went back to vacuuming snark blood.

Lindebaum sprung for the rice and they all gave snark vindaloo a try. After the first bite Lindebaum remarked that it had a sort of will-o-the-wisp flavour. Alan maintained that it tasted a lot like fishy-chicken, "Like I told you!" he reminded Stefan.

They finished it off, and, since neither one got sick or died, they declared it a success and began talking about how to fix the next dish.

"It's too bad that most of the beast vanished," Alan decided. "We could have eaten on the thing for months."

"Yeah, and saved a lot of money at the going price for protein out here on Ganymede," Lindebaum added.

After heated discussion they settled on Boojum stir-fry for the next meal, which they planned for a week later.

"It won't be the same without any fresh ginger," Stefan complained. But what was there to do out here on Ganymede?

It took three weeks to repair the damage wrought on Lindebaum's bedroom and bathroom. Some non-critical things simply weren't available on Ganymede and those would have to await the next space-freighter, tentatively scheduled in about six months.

Once things had been more or less repaired, Lindebaum finally had time to consider finishing the rest of 'Atchafalaya Boojum'. He retrieved the book one evening and went to bed to read it. It took a few minutes to figure out where he had left off and he had no sooner located his place than he heard a rustling noise in his closet. No one had pets on Ganymede, since the price of importing protein to feed them was too exorbitant, so that obviously wasn't what he was hearing.

There were a few rats now, descendants of some Norway rats that had snuck aboard in the cargo bays of some of the early flights, however. He pushed a security button and a minute later Alan rushed in, his laser sidearm armed and at the ready. Lindebaum had gotten out of bed and armed himself with a metre-long piece of pipe that he kept in the bedroom for just such occasions.

"What's up?" Alan asked.

"Something's in the closet. I heard it rummaging around. Probably a rat, but if it is it sounds like a really big one. "

"If you go over and jerk the door open I'll shoot whatever comes out."

"Okay. I'll open it on the count of three." He tip-toed over and grasped the handle. However, he only got as far as "two" when whatever it was inside the closet came right through the door with a loud roar, ripping it off of its hinges.

Lindebaum jumped back as it came out. Alan fired a volley of six quick laser bursts into the chest of what looked like a smaller version of the Boojum that had paid them an unwelcome visit a few weeks earlier. It landed at Alan's feet. Alan jumped back and then pumped three more beams into its head as a precaution.

Alan looked over at Lindebaum, who was holding his bat like a baseball player expecting the next pitch.

"I think maybe you have an infestation, Boss," Alan said.

Alan lowered his pipe and walked over to peer at the creature. "Yeah. It looks that way."

"This one looks a lot like the Boojum, but it's green not black, of course, and a lot smaller. I'd guess this one's only about 70 kilos."

"Lots of teeth, though," Lindebaum observed.

"Yeah. It could easily take off an arm if it got hold of one. Do you suppose it's going to vanish like the big one did?"

"I have no idea."

"I'm *not* cooking this one," Alan said. "I'm getting pretty tired of fishy-tasting Boojum meat. What do you want to do?"

"I don't know. Let's wait a few minutes and see what happens."

What happened next was that the youngster's mother came through the closet looking for it. Alan never even got his pistol up in time for a quick shot. The snark grabbed him by the throat and snapped his neck; he was dead in the blink of an eye. Lindebaum bolted out the door, slammed it shut and hit the alarm. When he reached the kitchen he was met by Stefan holding a particle beam weapon at the ready.

"Boojum!" Lindebaum yelled. They retreated behind the counter again and waited. Stefan set the intensity to high, a setting that he had never actually used, since it was powerful enough to penetrate 800-millimetre-thick armour.

When it came through the door Stefan blew its head off.

"Where's Alan?" he asked, looking around.

"Dead. In my bedroom."

"Dead? What happened?"

Lindebaum recounted the events. Stefan ran back down the hallway and into the bedroom to see for himself. He found Alan on the floor with his throat ripped out. Next to him was the dead immature Boojum.

"We either move out of here or I quit," Stefan told him.

"We're definitely moving," Lindebaum assured him. "We'll move into the Quantum Nights Hotel tonight. I believe there is a spaceship from Titania due into Ganymede in three days on its way back to Mars. I'll book us on it. Ganymede is much too dangerous for my comfort level. We may not survive the next time one of these things shows up."

"Good. Where do you think they come from?"

"I don't really know, but I have a hunch that they are coming from another dimension or universe; one that we don't have access to but that they somehow do. Some scientists think that it might be possible to step from one dimension into another through a weak spot or a gap in the space-time interface between two universes. Some theorists think that the soft spot may be due to localized excessive stress points that are able to literally tear the fabric of space-time perhaps due to an abnormally high warp in the space-time continuum, such as might occur due to the merging of several massive black holes. Perhaps they're right. But then again, perhaps they're just blowing smoke."

"I'm sorry I asked. Can we get out of here?"

"No. Just stay on alert. I need to get Ganymede Security over here and take a look. Alan's dead, so we can't just leave! I hope they get here in time to see at least one of the Boojums. If not, then they'll never believe us!" He phoned G.S. No fewer than ten G.S. vehicles arrived within the next fifteen minutes, all with teams armed to the teeth. Fortunately, the Boojums didn't vanish this time. Lindebaum told them what had happened, but didn't mention the first Boojum's appearance and vanishing. Things were complicated enough without bringing all of that up.

Lindebaum and Stefan weren't allowed to leave for the hotel for another three hours. Lindebaum packed a small bag with a few clothes and his Lewis Carroll collection while the police stood around gaping and prodding the carcasses.

Five days later Lindebaum and Stefan went aboard the ship that had come in from Titania. Lindebaum deposited his books in his cabin safe.

It wasn't until they were several weeks out towards Mars that he happened to meet Dayna. Even though he was not an officer he was allowed to drink in the Officer's Lounge, since he had paid for a First Class suite. She was sitting on a stool at the bar sipping Subtle Azzigoom when he sat down on the stool beside her. She recognized him instantly, but he had no clue as to her identity. He was the first to speak. "Hi," he said, "do you mind if I join you?"

Her first thought was to just leave without speaking, but decided to play along, since he obviously didn't have a clue about who she was. "I suppose not."

"My name's Lindebaum," he said; "Jon Lindebaum."

"Where are you from?" she asked without offering any personal information about herself.

"I've lived on Ganymede for the past twelve years. How about you?"

"I live aboard ship; not necessarily the same one all the time. I don't really have a home base. What's the point? My trips are too long to justify having a place."

"You must travel light."

"Yes. Very light. Everything I really need is available on board. I have a few changes of clothes; that's pretty much it."

"I'm heading for Mars, and travelling light as well."

"Why Mars?"

"Oh, other than Earth's moon it was the first to be colonized, so Mars had lots of people and development. More things to do and stores to shop in."

"What sort of shopping do you do? Anything special?"

"Books, mostly. I like old books. Mars is relatively close to Earth, so when books are discovered on Earth they most often pass through Mars on their way out to the other planets. There's a better chance of finding something I want. The last I heard there were five bookstores. That's a lot."

"What sort of books do you look for?"

"You'll probably think I'm silly if I told you."

"Not at all. Let me guess." She pretended to study him for a few minutes, as if she was trying to guess by his appearance.

"You don't look like the athletic type, so I'd say it's probably not sport."

"You're right. I've never cared a thing about sport."

"Your hands aren't beat up and you have clean fingernails, so I'd guess you aren't interested in working with your hands and making or fixing things. Am I right?"

"You're right! Very observant."

"So, let's see; you might be an artist, but I don't see a speck of paint anywhere on you, so that's out. But you might be an art dealer or collector. My first guess would be art books."

"No, but you're getting warmer."

"Now that phrase tells me that you like childish things."

"Why?"

"Oh, it means you like little games that children play. 'You're getting warmer!' 'No, now you're getting colder.' That one."

"Interesting," he said. "Yes, I like childish things."

"Okay, let's see; you like art and children's things. My guess would be that you like children's books. You're obviously wealthy or they wouldn't allow you in this lounge, so you probably like to buy old, expensive children's books."

"That's amazing! Have we ever met?"

"Not that I can remember. I usually hang around with younger guys, so it's unlikely."

"Hey! I'm not *that* old."

"Yes you are. You could be my father; maybe even my grandfather, but I think that would be pushing it."

"So what's your guess for my age?"

"What if I hit it on the head? Do you give prizes?"

He laughed. "Not usually, but I'll make an exception in your case."

"You'll have to show me your identification or I won't believe you."

"Done. And what do I win if you miss? Do you also give prizes?"

"I won't commit until I know what your prize is."

"₦10,000," he said.

She wasn't impressed. "Cheapskate! No wager."

"Whoa! What would you accept?"

She thought for a moment. "₦250,000. I can tell that you can afford it."

He winced, but realized that she was right. That would just be pocket change. "I won't accept the bet until I know what your prize will be. It has to be good enough to justify that sort of a bet."

She didn't really care if she won or lost. Either way he would fall into her hands. He had obviously managed to escape the Boojum that she had intended for him. Here was a second chance. "If I miss the mark I'll put on my best dress—the one that's slit down to here (she pointed) and up to here (she pointed again)—and bring a bottle of wine to your cabin. You can do with me whatever you like for six hours. I'm worth it."

He didn't have to think it over. "I accept."

They shook hands.

"So, what's your guess?"

Dayna figured he was 68, so she aimed low to feed his ego. She pretended to be thinking it over very carefully; taking her time. She pretended to start to say something and then didn't. More thinking. She took a deep breath and crossed her fingers as if she was trying very hard to get the right answer. "Okay," she finally said. "I'd say you are probably 59."

Lindebaum let out a whoop, as if he had just won the Interplanetary Sweepstakes. He stepped off of the stool and danced a little victory dance in a tight circle. Grinning ear to ear he sat back down and pulled out his wallet and identification, which he handed to Dayna. "I win!" he said.

You lose, she thought. *Big time!* Then she said, "Sixty-eight? What? No way!"

"Yes, my way! Thank you for the compliment. Don't let my age deceive you. I'm old, but not *that* old, if you get my meaning."

She smiled a seductive smile. "I get your meaning. Maybe I've won in spite of myself. What night would you like me to pay you a visit?"

"How about tonight?"

"How about tomorrow night? I might need to get a little sleep before the festivities. You don't want me to show up and just fall asleep, I would guess."

"Tomorrow will be fine. How's 20:00?"

"Fine."

"I'm already looking forward to it."

"Does our little bet allow me to make a small request?" she asked.

"Perhaps. What is it?"

"I'd like to see some of your children's books. Would you do that? I would really enjoy it."

"Absolutely. It will be my pleasure."

CHAPTER V

A Boojum Posy for Alison

*H*omicide Inspector Kentaro Momma, a slightly built, quiet man, and CSI Technician Gisela Wagenknecht of Martian Security made their way to Jon Lindebaum's cabin. Over the years they had worked as a team on a number of homicides and when they were alone with each other he affectionately called her "Sissy-Tech". Reaching their destination, they showed their badges to the burly Interplanetary Marine who had been ordered to meet them at Lindebaum's cabin to give them access. "Good day, Sergeant Ohayashi," Momma said to the marine.

"Good day, Sir." He turned to Wagenknecht. "Ma'am."

"We need for you to let us into the cabin," Inspector Momma told him.

"Yes, Sir. I'll need to see both of your badges." He held out his hand to Momma and then to Wagenknecht.

The marine briefly studied their photos and their faces. "Thank you, Sir!" he barked as he handed Momma's badge back to him. "Thank you, Ma'am," he said in a quieter tone to Wagenknecht and returned her badge. "I'll need to turn on the emergency air system to purge the nitrogen inside the cabin before you can enter, Sir. It will take about five minutes, Sir."

"I understand, Sergeant. Please, proceed."

The marine turned and punched a code into a small panel embedded in the wall next to the door. There was a faint humming noise as the lethally oxygen-deficient atmosphere was displaced. The room had been sealed under a nitrogen blanket to impede decay until the room could be investigated by a CSI Team once the spaceship had finally docked at Mars. While they waited Momma and Wagenknecht both slipped on disposable shoe covers, since they had been warned that there was a lot of blood on the floor in the cabin.

About five-minutes later a small green LED over the door came on, indicating that the oxygen concentration inside was above 19.5 percent. The marine opened the door and stepped back. "Sir, all clear, Sir!" he shouted at them.

"Thank you, Sergeant," Momma said as he and CSI Tech Wagenknecht stepped inside. When he flipped on the cabin lights they both flinched at the ghastly sight, in spite of the fact that they had expected blood. There had obviously been a horrific struggle in the close quarters of the small cabin. Still-bright red blood was practically everywhere, even sprayed across the ceiling. The nitrogen blanket had retarded decay and the scene looked almost fresh in spite of the fact that it had been sealed for several months. The only thing missing was the body, which had been removed and placed in a refrigeration unit pending their investigation.

Momma and Wagenknecht spent the next fifteen-minutes methodically looking at the scene, but initially couldn't find anything that would indicate what might have happened. "Sissy-Tech, please take samples of the blood at various locations. If we are lucky perhaps we will find some DNA that doesn't belong to the victim or Mr Lindebaum."

Wagenknecht opened her kit and set to work collecting blood samples. While she was down on her knees collecting one of them she spotted something. "Momma-san, look there," she said, pointing under the table. "A syringe!"

He came over and peered where she was pointing and saw the syringe, partially covered in a clotted pool of blood. "Excellent, Sissy-Tech! Excellent. Please analyse it to find out what it contained."

Wagenknecht dropped the syringe into a polythene bag. "Anything else, Momma-san?"

"Yes. Please dust the safe for fingerprints, though I doubt that whoever—or whatever—did this would be so foolish as to leave prints."

"You would think not, but one never knows." She went over and dusted the door and sides of the open, empty safe. "There are a large number of good prints, Momma-san."

"Good. I think we are through here for the time being, Sissy-Tech. Let's have a look at the body."

They went to the door and removed their bloodied shoe covers before stepping back out into the corridor. "Please reseal the room, Sergeant, and displace the atmosphere with nitrogen again."

"Sir, yes Sir."

Momma and Wagenknecht went directly to a lower level of the ship where there was a refrigeration room. They met another marine who had been sent to meet them there. They showed him their badges and he opened the walk-in freezer where they saw a body bag on a gurney. The room temperature was maintained at just above freezing so that the body would not be frozen in case an autopsy would be required.

Momma went over and unzipped the bag so that they could view the corpse.

"I knew Dayna," Gisela remarked. "Not very well, though. We had dinner together a few times over the years when she would pass through Mars on her way to some other place. You can't tell it now, but at one time she was very beautiful. Guys would literally walk right into walls when they saw her if she wasn't wearing one of those hideous jumpsuits the crew wears."

"I must take your word for it, Sissy-Tech. It is hard to recognize a faceless corpse." They both peered inside, where there was a hand, both feet and some of the torso, including some shattered ribs and a section of the spine.

"How could anyone have done this?"

He paused. "I don't believe that anyone did this," he said. "I have seen what insane people sometimes do to corpses and they never look like this! This corpse has been ripped apart."

"What do you mean that it wasn't anyone? Somebody had to do this!"

"No, I think that it would be more accurate to say that 'something' did this; not someone."

"Some *thing*? Like what? There are no lions, tigers, or bears onboard!"

"Or anywhere, for that matter," he agreed. "All the big predators have long been extinct on Earth."

"Then what?"

"I have some information that has not been revealed to the public. There is a worry about panic if it were to leak out."

"Really? What? Please tell me. I'm not 'the public'."

"I am not supposed to tell even you, but I think you need to know, since you are assigned to this case. You must swear to keep it confidential between you and me. Don't even write anything about it in your reports."

"OK! I swear!"

"I have access to a top secret report of a similar incident that happened recently on Ganymede. Two terrifying creatures— things that witnesses describe as looking like dinosaurs— attacked three people there. One of these managed to take one of the victims before the remaining two people managed to kill the creatures."

"Are you saying that there are dinosaurs on Ganymede?"

"No, they just looked like dinosaurs. I don't know what they are. The witnesses said that they literally appeared out of thin air in the middle of a room."

Gisela laughed. "Very funny! You're kidding me, right?"

"No, Sissy-Tech, I am very serious. Very serious indeed."

"Really?"

He nodded. "Take a wild guess and see if you can imagine the identities of the two survivors."

She thought for a while, then shook her head. "I honestly have no idea, Momma-san. Tell me."

"One of them is our Mr Jon Lindebaum. The other one is his bodyguard, an ex-military man who goes by the name Stefan. He was also on this ship when Specialist Keiner was killed. The person who was killed by the creature on Ganymede was another one of Lindebaum's bodyguards. Even more curious is the fact that this all happened inside Lindebaum's residential pod."

Wagenknecht's jaw dropped. "You're kidding!"

"No, I'm quite serious. Our Mr Lindebaum is up to his eyeballs in monsters and blood. Once you have the results back on your samples we need to have a talk with Mr Lindebaum. How long will it take to have the results?"

"We should have them back in the morning."

"That's fine. There's no real hurry. Neither Lindebaum nor Stefan can go anywhere. We're all stuck on Mars for the foreseeable future. There are no ships arriving or leaving for at least another two weeks. Just to cover all of the bases, check

Keiner's tissues for traces of whatever you find out was in that syringe you discovered back in Lindebaum's cabin."

The next morning Wagenknecht arrived at Momma's office. "Good morning, Momma-san," she said as she walked in.

"Ah, Sissy-Tech, good morning. Do we have results."

"Yes. All of the human blood belonged to Keiner."

"The human blood? What's that supposed to mean?"

"Most of the blood is an unknown type. We have no idea what animal it belongs to. No such DNA is in the system to compare it against. The fingerprints were all Lindebaum's, which makes sense, since that was his cabin. The syringe is interesting. It has traces of a rare poison."

"Which one?"

"It's a sort of toxic soup of arsenic-based chemicals. The venom is from an aquatic arsenic-based life form found in deep sub-surface pools on Ganymede. The life form looks like a hybrid of a fish and sea snake. It's blind, since there is no light at the depths where it lives."

"Anything else?"

"Yes. One of Keiner's fingerprints was on the syringe. None of the poison is detectable in her tissues or in the blood samples I collected."

"Very interesting! It would seem that Specialist Keiner might have intended to poison Lindebaum," Momma concluded. "But something terrible happened and she wound up dead instead."

Gisela nodded.

"It's time to interview Lindebaum."

They located Lindebaum and Stefan in a hotel in Sector 76. "Momma knocked on the door and Stefan answered, holding a laser pistol aimed at Momma's chest. "Can I help you?" he asked.

"I am Homicide Inspector Kentaro Momma and this is CSI Tech Gisela Wagenknecht. We are from Martian Security. We need to have a word with you and Mr Lindebaum. You need to immediately lower your weapon."

"Let's see your identification first," Stefan demanded.

They showed him their badges and Stefan lowered his weapon while stepping back to let them in. "Mr Lindebaum is in the living area. Follow me, please." He led the way.

Lindebaum was standing up when they entered the sitting area. Momma introduced themselves. "We need to talk with you about the incident that happened in your cabin en route from Ganymede to Mars on the night of the 26th of November."

"Of course. Please, have a seat." Lindebaum gestured at two chairs opposite the sedan welded to the metal floor.

When they were seated Momma took out a small recorder and turned it on. "Our conversation will be recorded. If I determine that either of you have lied to me then you will be arrested for perjury. Prison on Mars is far from pleasant, I can assure you. You have very few rights here. Do both of you understand?"

"Yes," Lindebaum said, and Stefan also replied in the affirmative.

"Mr Lindebaum, I want you to tell me what happened on the night that Specialist Dayna Keiner came to your room."

"We had met in the Officer's Lounge—"

"Excuse me. Are you an officer?" Momma asked.

"No, I just paid for the most expensive suite on the ship. One of the perks with that is access to the Officer's Lounge."

"I see. Go on."

"We had some drinks and talked. At one point we made a wager. She said that she could guess my age and wanted to bet on it. We agreed that if she could guess it then I would pay her a very large sum of money. If she missed it then she would spend the night with me in my cabin. She was a very attractive woman, I can assure you."

"Go on."

"She showed up at my cabin wearing a very provocative dress and with a bottle of wine. She had told me that she would like to see my collection of old books before things got livelier."

"Old books? She wanted to see your book collection?"

"Yes, I have a large collection of old editions of Lewis Carroll. She also liked old children's books. She wanted to see them."

"So, what happened then?"

"I went over and got the books out of the safe in the cabin—"

"You kept your old books in the safe?"

"Yes. They are very valuable."

"How valuable would that be? Just a rough guess."

"Oh, I suppose ten or fifteen million New Dollars; it's hard to say."

"Are you serious?"

"Yes. They are very rare."

"Please, go on."

"I came back with the books and sat them down on the table in front of her. She insisted on drinking some wine. She had already poured two glasses full while I was getting the books. She drank hers straight away, but I didn't."

"Why not?"

"I don't drink wine. It triggers migraines for me. I told her this. She looked very angry, but seemed to sort of get over it. She asked to let her see one of the books. I was surprised at the one she wanted to see."

"Which one was it?"

"An obscure one, about a Boojum."

"What is a Boojum?"

"It's a mythical beast that is a sub-species of snark. Snarks are just another kind of mythical beast. If you happen to encounter a Boojum snark then you supposedly suddenly vanish."

"Vanish?"

"Yes. Disappear."

"Tell me, Mr Lindebaum—this Boojum snark—does it by any chance look like a dinosaur?"

"In the book, yes. It's described as looking rather like a *T. rex*."

"Isn't it true that you encountered these beasts in your home on Ganymede?"

Lindebaum was quiet for a few minutes, thinking about what to say. "Yes. Two of them appeared in my residential pod. Alan, my other bodyguard, killed one of them right off. But the second one surprised him and killed him before he could shoot it. I ran into the kitchen area where Stefan was. He killed the second one. Right after this happened Stefan and I packed up and checked into a hotel, then caught the next ship out of Ganymede. It was returning to Mars, so that's why we're here. I didn't care where it was going as long as it was away from Ganymede and the monsters that evidently live there."

"So, let's get back to what happened in your cabin on this ship."

"Keiner insisted on reading the book about the Boojum. I could tell she was angry that I wouldn't drink any of her wine, so I decided to humour her while she read it. Curiously, she started to read it near the end of the story. Suddenly we all heard a deep growl from inside another room of my suite. I recognized what it was and so did she, it was as if she was expecting it to appear. She bolted for the door, but she never made it. This thing—this Boojum monster—snagged her as she tried to run by. Stefan, who was in another room, also heard the noise and knew what it was. We both ran towards a rear door but before we could escape it came charging at us.

Unfortunately, Stefan didn't have his particle beam weapon with him, so all he could do was shoot it in the head with the small laser weapon he always has on his hip. It wasn't powerful enough to kill it outright, but it was obviously wounded and bloodied. Then, suddenly—this is going to sound weird—it disappeared. Just like that! It vanished into thin air. We went back into where Keiner had been attacked. She was a mess—what little of her that was left. There was blood everywhere. We called security. They showed up and we changed cabins. They sealed the cabin pending a CSI investigation."

"That's us," Inspector Momma said.

"Yeah, I guessed that's what you were doing here."

"Had you ever met Keiner before?"

"It's strange that you should ask that. I don't recall ever meeting her, but there was something very familiar about her. Perhaps it was her voice. I'm not sure."

"This is probably going to be hard to believe, but I actually believe everything you've told me," Momma said.

"Really? Monsters appearing out of thin air and all?"

"Yes. Probably from an alternate universe, is my guess. Something about that book triggers them. Perhaps a single spoken sentence. Where is the book, by the way?"

"I've got it in that safe over there."

"I'd like to see it," Momma said.

"Certainly." Lindebaum went over and retrieved it. "Here you go."

Momma flipped through it, and thought for a few moments. "Do you have a particle-beam weapon, Stefan?"

"Yes."

"I assume that you're probably a reasonably good shot with it."

"Yeah. I'm certified as Marksman."

"Let's step outside. Bring your weapon. I'm going to read this book out loud. I want you to be at the ready and shoot anything that comes out of thin air. Can you do that?"

"Sure. Why not? I could use a little target practice."

"Good. Come on, let's go outside."

They all traipsed outside.

"Gisela, you and Mr Lindebaum get behind something substantial and stay out of the line of fire," Momma instructed, "just in case."

Everyone got in position and Momma started reading the book aloud, starting about two-thirds of the way through it. About thirty minutes into the story a thin black line appeared in the atmosphere. A moment later a Boojum charged through, its head held high as if smelling the air for scent. Stefan cut it in half with a single high intensity beam. To their shock, a few minutes later, two more Boojums suddenly burst through the rip. Stefan methodically blew their heads off.

Momma got on his phone and called Security for assistance. As he was on the phone another Boojum came through the rip, followed by an especially large one, presumably a male. Stefan dropped them too, but the big male almost made it to Stefan, crashing to the ground only three metres away from his feet. Its enormous jaws continued snapping in Stefan's direction for at least another minute or two as it slowly expired.

Inspector Momma suddenly got very worried. "My stars! What have I done?" he asked himself in a low voice. "What *have* I done?" To his horror the rip in the air did not reseal. At one place there was an obvious open gap through which it was actually possible to see what was on the other side. A fearless man, Momma walked over for a closer look. What he saw was an alien world with a heavily cratered, rocky surface. A reddish sun was low in the black sky, near the horizon. There were three visible moons, the largest of which had a purplish hue and a red accretion disc tilted at about 45 degrees to the horizon and towards the sun. At the base of a towering impact crater, about a hundred metres distant, Momma noticed movement and focusing there he saw a very large Boojum. It stopped and slowly turned to stare in his direction, as if it could see the rip or smell Momma's scent. It suddenly charged.

"Not good!" Momma thought.

CHAPTER VI

Oh, I've Gone to Boojumlandia with a Laser on My Knee!

*H*omicide Inspector Kentaro Momma ran for his life, sprinting away from the tear in the fabric of the space-time continuum that separated the universe containing the Milky Way Galaxy from whatever the unknown parallel universe on the other side included. "Incoming!" he yelled as he ran past Stefan, like an actor in one of those old World War II movies produced in the United States back in the late twentieth century. "A big one!" he added. Stefan set the power to maximum on his particle beam weapon before smoothly raising it to his shoulder, ready for whatever came through. He didn't have long to wait. A few seconds later the largest Boojum that they had yet seen smashed through the invisible fabric, triggering high-velocity concentric shock waves across the interfacial surface of the space-time continuum.

Momma, by this time cowering next to CSI Technician Gisela Wagenknecht behind a natural stone barrier, winced in horror at the deafening roar that came from the throat of the creature. Both he and Wagenknecht screamed. Moments later, the particle beam pulse from Stefan's weapon vaporized the top half of the Boojum's skull and the rest of its body smashed into the thick foundation of the pod cluster.

Stefan seemed unperturbed, even though the huge body had landed a mere eight metres away from where he was standing. He calmly strode over to the carcass and gave it a swift kick in a rib to see if it was still alive; it wasn't. Momma and Wagenknecht cautiously emerged from behind the barrier and went over to look at the creature's remains, staring in unbelief at the row of huge megalodon-size teeth that outlined the lower jaw. Out of curiosity, Wagenknecht cautiously tested the sharpness of the serrated edge of a large tooth with her forefinger and managed to nick it. "Yikes!" she yelped. "It's like a razor!"

Just then three security vans came screeching up, their blue lights flashing. Several squads of fully armed Interplanetary Marines and Martian Security personnel emerged with weapons at the ready. Momma hurried over to the officer who seemed to be ordering people around and read his nameplate. "Lt Malcolm, I am Martian Police Homicide Detective Kentaro Momma. We have a serious problem here," pointing at the huge carcass. He quickly briefed the Lieutenant about the immediate threat, gesturing at the rip that was now open enough for all of them to easily see through. "What's left of that monster just came through that rip from an alien world in what I believe to be a parallel universe! More creatures just like it will no doubt be coming through as well. You need to set up a killing field and annihilate them as they come through. They will not hesitate to eat us!"

"Where's the rest of its head?" Lt Malcolm asked.

Momma pointed at Stefan. "Vaporized. He blew its brains out. Look, you need to send an urgent request for construction workers and start building a five-metre-high ultra-strong barrier around this zone. There are probably thousands of creatures over there just like that one. We need to contain them until you can arrange to evacuate Mars."

"Evacuate Mars?"

"Yes. As soon as possible!"

"Are you out of your mind? There aren't enough spaceships in the entire fleet or places to take them in order to evacuate Mars. The last census I'm aware of listed over 400,000 people here on Mars! Get a grip, man!"

"What do *you* suggest then, Lt Malcolm?"

"At the moment, I only see three choices. If someone can figure out how to seal that rip they need to get at it. Alternatively, we can kill the monsters as they come through the gap. The third option is to send squads in through the rip and kill them on their own planet, or moon, or whatever it is over there."

"That could be a suicide mission. The creatures there—we're calling them Boojums—might overwhelm them, or else the rip might re-close on its own accord and leave the men stranded in that hostile alien world."

"I agree that the third option would be the last resort, but I have a feeling that it will probably be necessary in the end."

"Who would be willing to take such a risk? You couldn't order your men to do that!"

"I would be willing to lead a voluntary force. When my men understand what might happen to those here on Mars if they don't, then there will be more than enough heroes stepping forward. Some, like me, will want to go just for the adventure of it and the chance to kill huge dangerous animals, even when they know they might not return. Mars is a pretty dull and boring place for people trained to kill stuff."

At that very moment they all heard a terrifying roar as another Boojum emerged, jaws agape and charging hard. The marines cut it to ribbons.

"You need to tell me exactly what you know about that rip," Lt Malcolm told Momma. "Step over here out of the way of the crossfire and brief me! Bring your CSI sidekick along with you."

They stepped out of the way and Momma started telling him what he knew. Lt Malcolm patiently listened with an expressionless face until Momma had finished. "So, Inspector Momma, this is a fine mess that you've gotten us into."

"Well, in a way, I suppose I'm responsible for this present problem, but I didn't start this entire thing. That Keiner woman did! She's to blame!"

"I don't think so," Lt Malcolm said. "I think this is just one of many episodes that have happened over the millennia. It's not the first time and I'm betting it won't be the last time either."

Momma gave him a quizzical look. "What are you talking about?"

"Based on what I've heard so far, this is as good an explanation for quantum evolution as any I've ever heard."

"Meaning what?"

"Well, think about it. Over millions of years on Earth there were sudden extinctions of huge numbers of animals and plants. No real good explanations; not in mind my anyway. A bunch of wild guesses, if you ask me! However, we now have proof of the existence of life on parallel universes—well, on one, at least—so it's quite plausible that such rips have appeared repeatedly over the eons. A rip might only appear once in ten thousand-years, or even once in a hundred thousand-years, but over millions and millions of years those random events could have introduced creatures from other worlds multiple times. The invaders could have easily preyed upon and destroyed entire ecosystems and classes of existing animals on Earth, causing rapid extinctions. That thing over there sure looks like a dinosaur to me. Their big mistake this time is that we're smarter than they are and we're armed with formidable weapons, not sticks and stones. We won't be such easy pickings this time."

Momma wasn't convinced. "That all sounds like pseudo-science!"

Lt Malcolm shrugged. "Maybe. Anyway, there's also the other sides of the coin."

"A coin only has two sides," Momma said.

"A coin has a minimum of three sides. It's called the edge," he rebutted.

"Okay. But it can't have more than three."

"You're assuming that all coins are cylindrical. You ever hear of octagons? You need to step out of your ding-dang paradigm, Detective! Expand your mind!"

"Drop it!" Momma snarled. "I get your point. I'll allow that there may be multiple sides to a coin. We've got bigger problems here than this stupid argument about geometric solids!"

"Well, we're the big, bad monsters at this moment in time in this star system. We have snicker-snack particle beam weapons that can blow them away or cut them up into little pieces for Snark kebab. Shoot, we might want to consider invading their planet and taking it away from *them*. Hit 'em while they're sitting on the pot reading a Boojum joke book. In case you haven't noticed, Mars and the rest of the planets and moons in our solar system aren't exactly easy to colonize, and we're a long way away from developing interstellar travel capability. Shoot, we can't seem to get past the 155,000 kilometre per hour barrier! We ain't going anywhere at that poky speed! Obviously, that world we can see a bit of through that gap supports life. So far we've just seen a few big predators. But they're eating something over there, so there's got to also be smaller ones to snack on. Shoot, maybe we could even domesticate some of them. This one has red blood, so my guess is that there's an oxygen-rich atmosphere over there. The sky I can see at the moment's black, but my guess is that it's just night and not empty. That place might well support human life. What I'm suggesting is that we should go and colonize it while we have the opportunity. Now or never!"

"What if the rip re-closes before we can get an invasion force organized? Everything that I've heard about the rips indicates that they're very unstable."

"You've got the key to another world in your hand right there, Inspector Momma," he said, pointing at the copy of *In the Boojum Forest*. "I don't understand what it is about reading that 'Atchafalaya Boojum' story out loud that triggers it, but I guess it must be some series of just the right sounds. We can let 'er rip at will, wherever and whenever we want to. Just say the magic words! Presto!"

"There's another side of the coin," CSI Tech Wagenknecht interrupted. She had been patiently listening to the discussion and this was her first speech.

"Like what?" Lt Malcolm asked.

"We know that the rip is unstable. It usually closes on its own. So far, this one has stayed open for longer than the previous one, but it might close on its own accord with just the right disturbance. Or it just might be that this particular rip, which is now more like a door big enough to drive a dinosaur through, might just stay open permanently. What if we want or need it to close, but we can't figure out how to do it?"

"Why would that be so bad, once we've killed all of the Big Bad Boojums?" Lt Malcolm asked.

"Well, for one thing, what if the atmosphere over there began leaking out though this open door? Or worse, what if it started leaking out of hundreds or thousands of such holes that we elected to open up just so we could quickly invade Boojumlandia? It's conceivable that over time the entire atmosphere over there might literally seep through into Mars and from there into interplanetary space, depleting the oxygen in our new home."

"That would take a very long time. We could restrict the number of entry points we create. Or perhaps someone might figure out how to simply plug it. Super-space-glue or something."

"There might also be alien bacteria, viruses, or parasites that mankind would have no protection against," chimed in Inspector Momma. "Or what if there's something bigger and meaner over there that eats Boojums? Who knows? Boojums might not even be at the top of the food chain! There is a very long list of potential problems."

"We need to send in spies to reconnoitre, get samples for testing, and so on," argued Lt Malcolm. "Take a look around and see what's over there."

"You'll need a skilled technician to catch the samples," she said.

"True."

"I'll go," she said.

"You?" the Lieutenant asked, surprised.

"Yes. I'm not afraid and I have the skills. If I die over there then so be it. Death by Boojum would be almost instantaneous. One chomp and it's 'Hello, eternity!' The trauma would be so intense that you would just go numb for the few seconds it took until you bled out. There are worse ways to go—much worse."

"Like death by boredom?" Lt Malcolm asked.

"Yes."

Lt Malcolm turned away and walked over to a marine, who handed him his particle beam weapon, a power pack, a canteen, and a rations canister. Without so much as a wave good-bye he walked over to the rip and stepped through. Sissy-tech grabbed her CSI case and ran after him, darting through the rip without the least hesitation: the Adam and Eve of Boojumlandia.

Alice's Adventures in Wonderland, by Lewis Carroll, 2015

Through the Looking-Glass and What Alice Found There,
by Lewis Carroll 2009

Alice's Adventures in Wonderland, illus. June Lornie, 2013

Alice's Adventures in Wonderland, illus. Mathew Staunton, 2015

Alice's Adventures in Wonderland, illus. Harry Furniss, 2016

A New Alice in the Old Wonderland,
by Anna Matlack Richards, 2009

New Adventures of Alice, by John Rae, 2010

Alice Through the Needle's Eye, by Gilbert Adair, 2012

Wonderland Revisited and the Games Alice Played There,
by Keith Sheppard, 2009

Alice's Adventures under Ground, by Lewis Carroll, 2009

The Nursery "Alice", by Lewis Carroll, 2015

The Hunting of the Snark, by Lewis Carroll, 2010

The Haunting of the Snarkasbord, by Alison Tannenbaum,
Byron W. Sewell, Charlie Lovett, & August A. Imholtz, Jr, 2012

Snarkmaster, by Byron W. Sewell, 2012

In the Boojum Forest, by Byron W. Sewell, 2014

Murder by Boojum, by Byron W. Sewell, 2014

Close Encounters of the Snarkian Kind,
by Byron W. Sewell, 2016

Alice's Adventures in Wonderland,
Retold in words of one Syllable by Mrs J. C. Gorham, 2010

𐐈𐑊𐐮𐑅'𐑆 𐐈𐐼𐑂𐐯𐑌𐐽𐐲𐑉𐑆 𐐮𐑌 𐐎𐐲𐑌𐐼𐐲𐑉𐑊𐐰𐑌𐐼,
Alice printed in the Deseret Alphabet, 2014

Alice's Adventures in Wonderland,
Alice printed in Dyslexic-Friendly fonts, 2015

ALICE'S ADVENTURES IN A DYSLEXIC WONDER-LAND, *Alice* printed in a font that simulates Dyslexia, 2015

Alice's Adventures in Wonderland,
Alice printed in the Ewellic Alphabet, 2013

'Ælɪsɪz Əd'ventʃəz ɪn 'Wʌndəˌlænd,
Alice printed in the International Phonetic Alphabet, 2014

Alis'z Advnčrz in Wunḍland,
Alice printed in the Ñspel orthography, 2015

Alice's Adventures in Wonder-land, *Alice* printed in the Nyctographic Square Alphabet, 2011

·𐑨𐑤𐑦𐑕'𐑦𐑟 𐑩𐑛𐑝𐑧𐑯𐑗𐑼𐑟 𐑦𐑯 ·𐑢𐑳𐑯𐑛𐑼𐑤𐑨𐑯𐑛,
Alice printed in the Shaw Alphabet, 2013

ALISIZ ADVENCƎRZ IN WUNDRLAND,
Alice printed in the Unifon Alphabet, 2014

Elucidating Alice: A Textual Commentary on *Alice's Adventures in Wonderland*, by Selwyn Goodacre, 2015

Behind the Looking-Glass: Reflections on the Myth of Lewis Carroll, by Sherry L. Ackerman, 2012

Selections from the Lewis Carroll Collection of Victoria J. Sewell, compiled by Byron W. Sewell, 2014

Clara in Blunderland, by Caroline Lewis, 2010

Lost in Blunderland: The further adventures of Clara, by Caroline Lewis, 2010

John Bull's Adventures in the Fiscal Wonderland,
by Charles Geake, 2010

The Westminster Alice, by H. H. Munro (Saki), 2010

Alice in Blunderland: An Iridescent Dream,
by John Kendrick Bangs, 2010

Rollo in Emblemland, by J. K. Bangs & C. R. Macauley, 2010

Gladys in Grammarland, by Audrey Mayhew Allen, 2010

Alice's Adventures in Pictureland,
by Florence Adèle Evans, 2011

Eileen's Adventures in Wordland, by Zillah K. Macdonald, 2010

Phyllis in Piskie-land, by J. Henry Harris, 2012

Alice in Beeland, by Lillian Elizabeth Roy, 2012

The Admiral's Caravan, by Charles Edward Carryl, 2010

Davy and the Goblin, by Charles Edward Carryl, 2010

Alix's Adventures in Wonderland:
Lewis Carroll's Nightmare, by Byron W. Sewell, 2011

Álobk's Adventures in Goatland, by Byron W. Sewell, 2011

Alice's Bad Hair Day in Wonderland,
by Byron W. Sewell, 2012

The Carrollian Tales of Inspector Spectre,
by Byron W. Sewell, 2011

Alice's Adventures in An Appalachian Wonderland,
Alice in Appalachian English, tr. Byron & Victoria Sewell, 2012

Patimatli ali Alice tu Vãsilia ti Ciudii,
Alice in Aromanian, tr. Mariana Bara, 2015

Алесіны прыгоды ў Цудазем'і (Alesiny pryhody u Tsudazem'i), *Alice* in Belarusian, tr. Max Ščur, 2013

На тым баку люстэрка, і што там напаткала Алесю (Na tym baku liusterka i shto tam napatkala Alesiu), *Looking-Glass* in Belarusian, tr. Max Ščur, 2013

Ahlice's Aveenturs in Wunderlaant, *Alice* in Border Scots, tr. Cameron Halfpenny 2015

Alice's Mishanters in e Land o Farlies, *Alice* in Caithness Scots, tr. Catherine Byrne 2014

Crystal's Adventures in A Cockney Wonderland, *Alice* in Cockney Rhyming Slang, tr. Charlie Lovett, 2015

Aventurs Alys in Pow an Anethow, *Alice* in Cornish, tr. Nicholas Williams, 2015

Alice's Ventures in Wunderland, *Alice* in Cornu-English, tr. Alan M. Kent, 2015

آلیس در سرزمین عجایب (Âlis dar Sarzamin-e Ajâyeb), *Alice* in Dari, tr. Rahman Arman, 2015

La Aventuroj de Alicio en Mirlando, *Alice* in Esperanto, tr. E. L. Kearney, 2009

La Aventuroj de Alico en Mirlando, *Alice* in Esperanto, tr. Donald Broadribb, 2012

Trans la Spegulo kaj kion Alico trovis tie, *Looking-Glass* in Esperanto, tr. Donald Broadribb, 2012

Les Aventures d'Alice au pays des merveilles, *Alice* in French, tr. Henri Bué, 2015

Les Aventures d'Alice au pays des merveilles, *Alice* in French, tr. Henri Bué, illus. Mathew Staunton, 2015

ელისის თავგადასავალი საოცრებათა ქვეყანაში
(Elisis t'avgadasavali saoc'rebat'a k'veqanaši),
Alice in Georgian, tr. Giorgi Gokieli, 2016

Alice's Abenteuer im Wunderland,
Alice in German, tr. Antonie Zimmermann, 2010

Alice's Adventirs in Wunnerlaun,
Alice in Glaswegian Scots, tr. Thomas Clark, 2014

Balþos Gadedeis Aþalhaidais in Sildaleikalanda,
Alice in Gothic, tr. David Alexander Carlton, 2015

Nā Hana Kupanaha a ʻĀleka ma ka ʻĀina Kamahaʻo,
Alice in Hawaiian, tr. R. Keao NeSmith, 2012

Ma Loko o ke Aniani Kū a me ka Mea i Loaʻa iā ʻĀleka
ma Laila, *Looking-Glass* in Hawaiian, tr. R. Keao NeSmith, 2012

Aliz kalandjai Csodaországban,
Alice in Hungarian, tr. Anikó Szilágyi, 2013

Eachtraí Eilíse i dTír na nIontas,
Alice in Irish, by Nicholas Williams, 2007

Lastall den Scáthán agus a bhFuair Eilís Ann Roimpi,
Looking-Glass in Irish, by Nicholas Williams, 2009

Eachtra Eibhlíse i dTír na nIontas,
Alice in Irish, by Pádraig Ó Cadhla, 2015

Le Avventure di Alice nel Paese delle Meraviglie,
Alice in Italian, tr. Teodorico Pietrocòla Rossetti, 2010

L's Aventuthes d'Alice en Êmèrvil'lie,
Alice in Jèrriais, tr. Geraint Williams, 2012

L'Travèrs du Mitheux et chein qu'Alice y dêmuchit,
Looking-Glass in Jèrriais, tr. Geraint Williams, 2012

Las Aventuras de Alisia en el Paiz de las Maraviyas,
Alice in Ladino, tr. Avner Perez, 2014

Alisis pīdzeivuojumi Breinumu zemē,
Alice in Latgalian, tr. Evika Muizniece, 2015

Alicia in Terra Mirabili,
Alice in Latin, tr. Clive Harcourt Carruthers, 2011

Alisa-ney Aventuras in Divalanda, *Alice* in Lingua de Planeta
(Lidepla), tr. Anastasia Lysenko & Dmitry Ivanov, 2014

La aventuras de Alisia en la pais de mervelias,
Alice in Lingua Franca Nova, tr. Simon Davies, 2012

Alice ehr Eventüürn in't Wunnerland,
Alice in Low German, tr. Reinhard F. Hahn, 2010

Contoyrtyssyn Ealish ayns Çheer ny Yindyssyn,
Alice in Manx, tr. Brian Stowell, 2010

Ko Ngā Takahanga i a Ārihi i Te Ao Mīharo,
Alice in Māori, tr. Tom Roa, 2015

Dee Erläwnisse von Alice em Wundalaund,
Alice in Mennonite Low German, tr. Jack Thiessen, 2012

The Aventures of Alys in Wondyr Lond,
Alice in Middle English, tr. Brian S. Lee, 2013

L'Avventure d'Alice 'int' 'o Paese d' 'e Maraveglie,
Alice in Neapolitan, tr. Roberto D'Ajello, 2016

L'Aventuros de Alis in Marvoland,
Alice in Neo, tr. Ralph Midgley, 2013

Ailice's Anters in Ferlielann,
Alice in North-East Scots, tr. Derrick McClure, 2012

Æðelgýðe Ellendǽda on Wundorlande,
Alice in Old English, tr. Peter S. Baker, 2015

Die Lissel ehr Erlebnisse im Wunnerland,
Alice in Palantine German, tr. Franz Schlosser, 2013

Alice Contada aos Mais Pequenos,
The Nursery "Alice" in Portuguese, tr., Rogério Miguel Puga, 2015

Соня въ царствѣ дива (Sonia v tsarstvie diva):
Sonja in a Kingdom of Wonder,
Alice in facsimile of the 1879 first Russian translation, 2013

Охота на Снарка (Okhota na Snarka),
The Hunting of the Snark in Russian, tr. Victor Fet, 2016

Ia Aventures as Alice in Daumsenland,
Alice in Sambahsa, tr. Olivier Simon, 2013

'O Tāfaoga a 'Ālise i le Nu'u o Mea Ofoofogia,
Alice in Samoan, tr. Luafata Simanu-Klutz, 2013

Eachdraidh Ealasaid ann an Tir nan Iongantas,
Alice in Scottish Gaelic, tr. Moray Watson, 2012

Alice's Adventchers in Wunderland,
Alice in Scouse, tr. Marvin R. Sumner, 2015

Mbalango wa Alice eTikweni ra Swihlamariso,
Alice in Shangani, tr. Peniah Mabaso & Steyn Khesani Madlome, 2015

Alice's Adventirs in Wonderlaand,
Alice in Shetland Scots, tr. Laureen Johnson, 2012

Alice muNyika yeMashiripiti,
Alice in Shona, tr. Shumirai Nyota & Tsitsi Nyoni, 2015

Ailice's Àventurs in Wunnerland,
Alice in Southeast Central Scots, tr. Sandy Fleemin, 2011

Alis bu Cëlmo dac Cojube w dat Tantelat,
Alice in Ṣurayt, tr. Jan Beṭ-Ṣawoce, 2015

Alisi Ndani ya Nchi ya Ajabu,
Alice in Swahili, tr. Ida Hadjuvayanis, 2015

Alices Äventyr i Sagolandet,
Alice in Swedish, tr. Emily Nonnen, 2010

Ailis's Anterins i the Laun o Ferlies,
Alice in Synthetic Scots, tr. Andrew McCallum, 2013

'Alisi 'i he Fonua 'o e Fakaofo',
Alice in Tongan, tr. Siutāula Cocker & Telesia Kalavite, 2014

Alice's Carrànts in Wunnerlan,
Alice in Ulster Scots, tr. Anne Morrison-Smyth, 2013

Der Alice ihre Obmteier im Wunderlaund,
Alice in Viennese German, tr. Hans Werner Sokop, 2012

Ventürs jiela Lälid in Stunalän,
Alice in Volapük, tr. Ralph Midgley, 2016

Lès-avirètes da Alice ô payis dès mèrvèyes,
Alice in Walloon, tr. Jean-Luc Fauconnier, 2012

Anturiaethau Alys yng Ngwlad Hud,
Alice in Welsh, tr. Selyf Roberts, 2010

I Avventur de Alìs ind el Paes di Meravili,
Alice in Western Lombard, tr. GianPietro Gallinelli, 2015

Alison's Jants in Ferlieland,
Alice in West-Central Scots, tr. James Andrew Begg, 2014

Di Avantures fun Alis in Vunderland,
Alice in Yiddish, tr. Joan Braman, 2015

Insumansumane Zika-Alice,
Alice in Zimbabwean Ndebele, tr. Dion Nkomo, 2015

U-Alice Ezweni Lezimanga,
Alice in Zulu, tr. Bhekinkosi Ntuli, 2014